"Everyone knows which woman I want in my life."

"And who might that woman be?" Holly asked.

Jim pushed her hair back and cupped her cheek, then bent his head as if to kiss her. "She's someone I probably don't deserve. You," he whispered. "Only ever you."

Holly reached up to wrap her arms around his neck, but he pulled back and turned half away. "This is a bad idea," he said with a quaver in his voice.

"You sound afraid. Of me?" Holly noted her voice wasn't all that steady, either.

He looked at her, the expression in his hazel eyes intense and grave. "Afraid? Me? Holly, I'm terrified."

Books by Kate Welsh

Love Inspired

For the Sake of Her Child #39
Never Lie to an Angel #69
A Family for Christmas #83
Small-Town Dreams #100
Their Forever Love #120

KATE WELSH

A two-time winner of Romance Writers of America's coveted Golden Heart Award, Kate lives in Havertown, Pennsylvania, with her husband of thirty years. When not at work in her home office creating stories and the characters that populate them, Kate fills her time in other creative outlets. There are few crafts she hasn't tried at least once or a sewing project that hasn't been a delicious temptation. Those ideas she can't resist grace her home or those of friends and family.

As a child she was often the "scriptwriter" in neighborhood games of make-believe. Kate turned back to storytelling when her husband challenged her to write down the stories in her head. With Jesus so much a part of her life, Kate found it natural to incorporate Him into her writing. Her goal is to entertain her readers with wholesome stories of the love between two people the Lord has brought together and to teach His truths while she entertains.

Their
Forever
Love
Kate Welsh

Published by Steeple Hill Books™

STEEPLE HILL BOOKS

Steeple
Hill™

ISBN 0-373-87126-0

THEIR FOREVER LOVE

Copyright © 2000 by Kate Welsh

This edition published by arrangement with Steeple Hill Books.

® and TM are trademarks of Steeple Hill Books, used under license.
Trademarks indicated with ® are registered in the United States Patent
and Trademark Office, the Canadian Trade Marks Office and in other
countries.

Visit us at www.steeplehill.com

Printed in U.S.A.

Trust in the Lord with all your heart,
And lean not on your own understanding.
In all your ways acknowledge Him,
And He shall direct your paths.
—*Proverbs* 3:5-6

To John. My hero. My husband. A man strong enough to give his heart and his life to Jesus.

I'd like to thank Chief Petty Officer (retired) John M. Krawchuk for sharing his expertise and experience on the U.S. naval presence in New Zealand and in the Antarctic, and both he and his wife, Debbie, for their invaluable help. Any errors are certainly mine and not theirs.

Chapter One

Eight-year-old Ian Dillon smiled in triumph as he entered the side door of First Fruits Church. He'd made it. And it had been as easy as he'd remembered. His last trip across town on the bus had been with his mother last winter to see the ice show. That was the day he'd noticed the church with the weird-sounding name. Which just went to prove what his pastor always told them. Nothing happens without a reason.

Ian scurried toward the sound of voices down a long hall, and through the double doors into the back of the sanctuary. The people were singing this really cool song that didn't sound like a God song. Then he listened to the words, and realized that it was a God song after all.

Wanting to go unnoticed, Ian moved toward a sign that pointed upward to the balcony. He crept up the stairs, and settled into a front row seat. Oh, this was going to be grand!

When the band stopped, a man on the stage greeted everyone, and welcomed them. It seemed as if Ian had arrived just in time because the smiling man said he had a special guest to get everyone started on a positive note that day. He said the guest was Jim Dillon. Ian's dad. A man Ian had wanted to meet all his life.

"Pastor Jim Dillon's church, the Tabernacle, is a rapidly growing congregation in horse country outside Philadelphia. I was there the night Jim accepted Jesus into his heart. He started changing Jim's life right there and then. Jim's come up here today to share some of those changes with you. Jim?"

Ian felt as if his eyes would bug out as the tall dark-haired man jogged up the steps from the front row! *No wonder Mum married him. He looks like a movie star!* Ian had noticed over the years that ladies always like men who looked like movie stars. The quiet applause stopped, and Ian leaned forward not wanting to miss a word.

"I am Jim Dillon. And I am an alcoholic."

Wow, Ian thought as he took a moment to look down at the people staring up at his father. Now he knew what his nanny meant about being able to hear a pin drop in a crowd. Ian knew what an alcoholic was. His mum had explained all about people who couldn't drink because if they did they couldn't stop until they were drunk. Ian saw people like that on the streets of New York sometimes. It was sad.

Then his father went on. "My road to sobriety started when I wandered—no—let's call it what it was—I *staggered* into a neighborhood mission. I was drunk, and just looking for a free meal.

"I am an alcoholic," he said again. "I will be an alcoholic on the day I die. But I won't drink. Not today. I don't even want to anymore. And with God's help, when I wake up tomorrow, I'll feel the same way.

"I don't claim that memories of those days, when a bottle was all I thought about, still don't hurt. Or that the futility of those years doesn't still fill me with shame, when I think of the mistakes I made.

"I grew up poor and rough, but I graduated high school, then enlisted in the navy. Entertainment became drinking with my buddies after work. That entertainment soon became a way of life for me. Then I met Holly."

Ian could hear wonder and what sounded to him like love in his father's voice. Why had Mum not come with Jim Dillon to America if he still loved her?

"A sweeter, gentler woman has yet to be born," his father continued in that same loving tone. "She was a princess, and I was going to be her Prince Charming. She even called me that. I married her, but by then the alcohol had me no matter how hard I tried not to drink. I messed up my marriage in a little over a year. I lost Holly and Ian, my beautiful baby son, who I haven't seen since he was six weeks old."

Now what sounded like tears mingled into his tone. "When Holly told me it was over, I let her go, because I was so ashamed of the way I'd failed her. I've regretted that decision every day of my life since.

More, I've regretted the sins I committed that made Holly need to leave to keep our son safe from my irresponsibility." He made a gesture with the back of his hand, that Ian was sure wiped away a tear, and Ian gripped the edge of his seat. He wanted to shout out that it was okay now, and that Ian forgave him, and Mum would, too.

"After losing them, life held little for me but pain and emptiness. And so I drank more and more, trying to kill the pain with what was the cause of it. I'd lost everything else by the time I dropped into a chair at the mission that night in Riverside.

"But before the free meal I had to sit through a sermon. For some reason I listened. And I learned that there was a way out of the bottle I lived in. That *way* was the Way, the Truth, and the Life. That way was Jesus Christ.

"I thank Him for what He's done in my life, and for the ways He's allowed me to serve Him and His people. And He keeps on giving. Remember my wife Holly and my son Ian back in New Zealand half a world away? I've tried to find them for years. I went back to New Zealand twice, but I was never able to find a trace of them...nor has Holly's father, who still lives there, heard from them.

"Recently I shared my heartache with a friend who's really into computers. He suggested that I post a notice to Holly and Ian on the Internet at a site for parents and children trying to find one another."

Ian stood and gripped the front rail of the balcony. His father was talking about him again!

"A month ago I got this e-mail message," Jim Dillon told the small group of men and women as he reached into his pocket. When he pulled out a piece of paper and started to read, Ian couldn't believe his ears.

Dear Jim Dillon,

I found you on a Web page by searching "find parent." I am hoping you might be my father because you sound so grand. I am eight years old. I live with my mother in New York City, but I was born in New Zealand where you say you lived when your son was born. Mum is a trade specialist with the New Zealand delegation to the United Nations. My father was a Yank in the American navy. When he left the country, my mother didn't go with him. I don't know why. Just that they decided that was best. I don't think it was. I want to know my father.

Are you him?

Please write back with some things about yourself and me. That way maybe we could be sure if I'm you're son and you're my father.

Ian Dillon

"I'd just about given up. And now He's given me this. There's more work to do. I haven't seen Ian, though I think I'm coming to know him pretty well through our correspondence. So far Holly has only given her permission for us to correspond. I think she's still too leery of me and the change in my life to feel comfortable about Ian seeing me. I really can't blame her. I wasn't husband or father of the year by any stretch of the imagination. But I pray every day that God will change her mind about letting me see him. I figure if He can help me find Ian half a world from where I was looking—him being here in New York City not New Zealand—then He can soften Holly's heart.''

Ian turned, and walked back to his seat. As quietly as possible, he picked up the sack he'd brought along with pictures of himself and his mum from when he was growing up, crept down the steps, and out into the hall. His father was still talking, but Ian knew he couldn't stay any longer. He knew he'd made a mistake. He should have waited until his mum changed her mind. He should have let God change it for her. He had to get home before he spoiled everything.

"Hey, kid! What are you doing in here?" a big man in a uniform shouted as he stalked down the hall. The man grabbed Ian by his backpack full of treasures.

Ian panicked. "You better turn me loose. My father won't like you manhandling me.''

"Oh? And who's your father, kid?" the man asked as he started to drag Ian along to some unknown destination. "I don't see him with you. All I see is a kid sneaking around a church where he doesn't belong. I don't recognize you, and I know all the kids who come here.''

"I'm Ian Dillon. My father was just talking about me onstage. He'll be real mad if you hurt me!''

The man stopped and let go of Ian. He pointed at a door to the right. "Then you get in there where you belong. I don't like kids wandering around alone. It isn't safe."

Ian hesitated. If he went back in, his father might see him, and his plan to just go back home and wait for God to fix everything would be ruined.

"Go on. Get!" the man growled.

Ian got! In a hurry. He tore through the door and noticed that now someone new was talking. Then he ran smack into a tall man in blue jeans. "Whoa, there, little fella. Where are you headed in such a hurry?" Ian didn't even have to look up. Even without the aid of the microphone, he recognized the voice he'd waited a lifetime to hear.

He sighed. Well, in for a penny in for a pound as Mum always said. "I came to see you," he said and stepped back to look up at his father. Ian almost gasped. He looked even more like a movie star close up than he had standing up front talking or in the picture on the Tabernacle's Web site. His hair was as dark as his own, but a bit less wavy, and his eyes were the same not-blue, not-brown, not-green shade as his own.

"I'm Ian, sir."

His father steered him back into the hallway, then he dropped to one knee. There were tears in his eyes. "You sure are, Son. You look just like I did at your age."

Jim stared at the image of himself from years ago when times were tough, and his life was frightening.

As he reached out and touched the boy's cheek, he'd never been so grateful that he'd met Holly. Because there was a marked difference in this boy's eyes from the ones that had once stared back at him from a dirty, cracked bathroom mirror. There was no hunger or disillusionment in these bright hazel eyes. Only trust and wonder.

"How did you know I'd be here?" Jim asked.

"My teachers say I'm quite a genius with the Web. I looked for a Web site for your church and I found one. It said you were coming here to speak today."

"Does a big boy of eight, who's a genius with computers, think it's too babyish for a son to hug his father?" Jim asked this child he could hardly remember holding as an infant.

"Probably," Ian said, and shrugged, "but I don't really care. I want a hug...Dad."

Jim waited not a second longer to scoop his son up into his arms the way he'd wanted to for eight long years. "Oh, you feel so good," he sighed as he hugged his child close.

Ian giggled as Jim stood still with him in his arms. "You're squashing me. Oh! I've never been held up so high. This is so grand!" Ian's arms wrapped around Jim's neck and squeezed.

"And you're strangling me!" Jim said.

This time they both laughed. It was a wonderful sound—his laughter blending with his son's. Jim closed his eyes, *Oh, Lord, You're so good to me.*

"Who might this young man be?" Harry Jordan,

the pastor of First Fruits Church asked as he came out into the hall.

"This, Harry, is my son Ian and this…" He looked around for the first time for Holly. "Ian, where's your mother?" he asked, dreading the answer. Did Holly hate him so much that she wouldn't even come inside the church?

"Uh…" the boy stammered, looking guilty.

Oh, he didn't want this. He didn't want Ian caught between his parents. "It's okay if she doesn't want to see me. I understand. I hurt her very badly. As long as she brought you here to see me today, it'll have to be enough."

Ian cast his eyes down. "Well…it isn't exactly like that."

"Did she drop you off and just leave you here?" That didn't sound either safe or like something his Holly would do.

"Not exactly," Ian answered.

Jim set him down in the hall and went down on his knee again so he'd be eye level with his son. "What exactly? She does know you're here, doesn't she?"

Ian looked up. "Oh, I didn't lie to her about today. I remembered what you said about me being truthful. I told her I was coming here."

"She couldn't have let you travel alone across New York City by yourself?"

"Not exactly."

"Then what exactly?" Jim asked, getting worried now.

"Well, I sort of left her a note telling her I was off to see you."

For the first time Jim noticed the backpack on the floor. "You ran away?"

"Oh, no. I'll just take the crosstown bus back after we've had our visit. That's how I got here. It was dead easy. I just took the bus that runs across Twenty-Third Street, and got off here at the corner."

Jim looked up at Harry, knowing there was horror written on his features, and saw it reflected on his friend's, as well. "I'll drive you there," Harry said without hesitation. "If the mother has called the police, you shouldn't just walk in there alone. You might need a witness that you knew nothing about Ian's plans ahead of time, and I'm pretty well-known to the police. They just might take my word and not haul you straight off to jail."

"Thanks. I owe you one."

"Ja-jail! Why—why would they do that?" Ian stammered.

"They could think I kidnapped you, son."

Big fat tears welled up and overflowed Ian's eyes. His lower lip puckered. "I came here to fix it so I could have a dad. Now I made it worse."

Jim squeezed the boy's shoulder. "Don't worry. Harry and I will straighten everything out. What is your phone number? We'll call your mum so she doesn't worry."

Ian hesitated. Jim could see his son's quick mind rethinking his position. "I don't think that's a good idea," Ian said.

"Oh, and why not?"

"Because if you take me there before she knows I've gone then she won't have to know."

"But she will because I'll tell her. She has a right to know you traveled halfway across the city alone."

"Then we best be off so she won't have so long to worry."

"You aren't going to give me the number, are you?" Jim asked.

Ian shook his dark head. "I don't think so. I know her better than you do. This is better."

"We should call, but I don't have time to argue the point with you now. We'd better get a move on before she calls out the National Guard to look for you."

Chapter Two

"Listen to me, Captain," Holly cried, "I don't care if you have to call out your National Guard to find my son. Just find him. Please. He's only a little boy, and he's out there all alone."

"Ma'am, I understand how upset you are—"

"No. No, you don't!" Holly wiped her eyes with the officer's handkerchief. "I don't think you have a clue how I feel. My little boy may be lost in New York City. If he arrived at the Port Authority safely, he planned to get on a bus to another city, in another state. A state almost half as big as all of New Zealand! Are you certain the officers at the terminal have Ian's picture?"

"Mrs. Dillon, we got on this immediately. Believe me. Are you sure he was headed for the Port Authority Terminal?"

Holly fought back tears at the thought of that huge

terminal and the kinds of things that could happen to her child there. "It's the only thing that makes sense. His note said he was going to see his father. His father lives somewhere in a county rather far out from Philadelphia, Pennsylvania. Ian took his savings with him, but it wasn't enough for a plane ticket or even train fare. It certainly wasn't enough for a cab or limo to take him that far. I just don't understand—"

A loud knock at the door drew her attention, and she pivoted toward it only to hear the most wonderful, querulous sound of her entire life. "I told you I have my key," Ian snapped as the door swung inward.

Holly rushed across the parlor. "Ian! Are you all right? Has anyone hurt you? I've been so terrified." She hugged him tight, never wanting to let him go, but he squirmed, so she did let go, remembering his recent quest for dignity.

"Sorry to have worried you, Mum. I did write a note. And I'll be fine, once you tell that bobby to unhand my father!"

She looked up from her son's precious face only to be confronted with the familiar yet distant scene of Jim Dillon being delivered to her home in the handcuffs by a police officer. Her heart kicked painfully, and her eyes drank in the sight of his handsome face.

He's alive! He's safe. Her first thoughts startled and frightened her. She'd wondered about him—yes. But in the abstract. Or so she'd told herself. There were times when dreams of the man she'd married, but hadn't been able to help, haunted her. She'd always awaken feeling guilty to have given up, but then she'd remind herself that Ian had to come first. Yet she'd still worried about what had become of him. Her last memory of Jim Dillon was of an angry broken man. This Jim, standing before her now, looked different…and it was more than his not being intoxicated.

"You know this man, ma'am?" the officer asked, distracting her from her confused introspection.

"I told you, he's my father! His friend told you, too!" Ian shouted. "He was bringing me home!"

Holly steeled herself. It was Ian who was important. It had been about him from the night he was born, when Jim wasn't there. And now with only a cyberspace link between them he'd somehow persuaded her son to disobey her. She could suddenly barely hold on to her fury. "He's the boy's father all right, though what he's doing with my son I can only imagine."

"He came to see me, Holly," Jim said in that same soft baritone voice that still visited her in her dreams.

Nightmares. They're nightmares, she told herself sternly.

"I'm sorry you've been worried," he continued. "I brought him home the second I realized that you weren't with him. I'd have called, but for some reason he wouldn't give me your number."

"It's true, Mum. Please don't be angry with him," Ian begged.

Holly took a deep calming breath. She could handle this. She handled difficult trade negotiations all the time. This would be a piece of cake. "Officer, thank you all for your efforts. This seems to be a private matter from here on out."

"You don't want to file a complaint?" the captain asked as the other officer freed Jim's hands.

"I did it all by myself!" Ian told him. "Dad asked about Mum, but I wouldn't give him the number. I wanted her to see how wonderful he is so I could go on seeing him. Please, Mum."

"Ian, that's quite enough," Holly said. "Go to your room, and let me deal with this. But make no mistake, we'll deal with your disobedience later."

"But, Mum…"

"Now, Ian James Dillon!"

"But—"

"It's okay, Son," Jim assured him. "You go on along. We'll talk soon. I promise."

Maddeningly, Ian ran to Jim, hugged him around his waist, then ran to his room.

Ian's gesture of affection frightened her beyond words. A flash of memory—two small coffins, two lovely children dead because of a drunken parent—stiffened her resolve. She couldn't let Ian end up that way. Holly forgot her compassion. She forgot the forgiveness she'd decided years ago to grant her ex-husband in absentia. She forgot the years of wondering and worrying about the man she'd worshiped then discarded, when life with him had become too hard.

Holly gestured the two policemen toward the door. "As I said, this is a private matter now. Thank you again for all your efforts." She escorted them out the door then shut it. Her anger had cooled not a degree in spite of the pause. Holly pivoted toward Jim.

"How dare you stroll into his life and act as if you have a right to be a father to him?" Holly demanded as she turned from the door, still gripping the door-knob tightly behind her back.

"Holly, if you'll just listen to reason. I had no idea he'd try to come see me alone. I didn't even tell him I'd be in New York. He got the information off my church's Web site."

"I don't know whether to believe you or not. All I've ever heard from you is lies. Why should I believe you now?"

"Because I'm not the same man, Holly. Ian must have told you that I have Jesus in my life now, and that I pastor a church. I only want to be a father to my son. I can be a good father now, Holly. I have something to offer Ian that I didn't before. You don't have to worry about me drinking again. I don't even have that desire anymore."

"Right. As if I haven't heard that before. My mother was sober for eight years and at the church nearly every day of her married life. A good little pastor's wife, doing her Christian duty. But then the nightmare started all over again. My father covered up her drinking for years, until she killed herself and my brother and sister. She drove them off a cliff while you were wintering over."

Jim nodded. "I heard about it a few years later. I'm sorry about Alan and Christie, Holly. I know you practically raised them. Their deaths must have been devastating. And I'm sorry your mother never changed, but I'll never drink again. I haven't had a drink in six years. I swear.''

"I don't care if you swear on a stack of Bibles. I don't care that you're a pastor. I don't care if you're in line to be the next pope! You are *not* seeing or talking to my child again. You signed away any right to him years ago.''

"I signed the divorce papers *you* filed. I never even read them. I wasn't capable of understanding anything the day I did it. If I gave up my rights, I never meant to.''

"You deserved to lose him. Your negligence nearly killed him. Suppose I hadn't found someone to take us to the hospital? It was the middle of the night and where were you when he had that first asthma attack? Out getting drunk instead of home with your family where you belonged.''

"You will never know how that night has haunted me. I gave in to your wishes for a divorce, but I didn't expect you to disappear without a trace!"

"After you—''

"Please don't!'' Ian cried from the hall doorway, then tried desperately to suck in some air. Holly felt her stomach drop. *Not another asthma attack. This is the sixth this month.*

"Ian!'' Jim called out as he shot across the room. He got to Ian before she could and scooped him up into his arms.

Ian weakly tried to circle Jim's neck with his arms. "I'm sorry, Dad. I only wanted…to fix it!''

"It's okay," Jim assured Ian then he turned toward her. "Holly, what's wrong with him? What should we do?"

Holly was surprised by the alarm reflected in Jim's eyes and voice. She knew in that instant that this was not a whim with him. He really cared about Ian and wanted to be a father to him. She'd thought he would tire of the novelty, and it would be easy to keep him out of her son's life. Clearly this wouldn't be easy at all.

Ian sucked another desperate breath, and she pushed away all but the concern of the moment. Jim's palpable panic. The first rule of caring for an asthmatic was to stay calm. "He has asthma," she said slowly. "Put him on the sofa, and calm down. Seeing you panic won't help him. Ian, did you use your rescue inhaler?" she asked her son as Jim laid him down and stepped reluctantly back.

Ian nodded, and gasped again. Holly still spoke calmly. "His inhaler is in his room, Jim. Do you know what one looks like?" He nodded. "Good. His room is the second door down the hall. It should be on his nightstand. Go get it," she ordered, and heard Jim hurry away.

"We'll try one more hit, when Jim gets back with it. All right?"

Ian grabbed her sleeve and pulled her near. "Mum, I'm...sorry. I really...went to see Dad...all on my own. You can even read our e-mails. Please don't...put him in jail."

She smoothed the hair of his sweaty forehead.

"The police have already left, poppet. And I'd never put your father in jail." She looked up into Jim's intense gaze, then took the inhaler he held out.

The inhaler failed to do any good, so she switched to the use of a mini nebulizer, but soon Holly could see that Ian's breathing had continued to degrade. She looked up at Jim, wishing for a split second that he'd always been there at moments like this. "I think he needs to be in hospital. Will you call a cab?"

"I have a car downstairs. The guy who invited me to speak at his church drove me here and left his car with me. Let's just get him there."

About to tell the man that his presence wasn't necessary, she glanced at her ex-husband and could only stare. He stood stiffly staring at Ian. And in those hazel eyes that she'd once been so drawn to, Holly saw such stark terror that her heart skipped. "Ta," she said automatically, thanking him even knowing that later it would grate on her sense of pride.

Jim blinked and nodded. Holly watched him mask the terror she had seen only seconds earlier, and she knew he'd done it for his son's sake. It irked her no end that he was Ian's father and that he was there. Somehow. Some way he'd managed to get into Ian's life. She had to find a way to force him back out before he hurt her precious son more than he already had.

Without uttering a single word, Jim carried Ian to the car, and put him into her arms as soon as she settled into the back seat. As he climbed in behind the wheel, Holly gave him directions, and they were on their way. In the rearview mirror she noticed that his lips were moving as he wove his way through traffic.

Is he praying? she wondered, then stiffened her resolve again. So what if he is? she scoffed. That proved nothing to her. Her father had prayed endlessly but he'd still failed his children miserably. Jim was no different.

But he said he had Jesus in his life, a small voice called to her from within. He hadn't used some general term like God. The people at her father's church had worshiped God on the Sabbath then had ignored Him and His tenets Monday through Saturday. She'd never heard anyone profess belief in the name of the Savior and not mean it. That could only mean that Jim had made greater changes in his life than she'd ever believed possible.

The ride to Cornell Medical Center was short, and soon the staff whisked Ian into pediatrics for treatment. At first Holly hated that she'd be left alone with Jim. She thought he'd use the time to try to change her mind about his relationship with Ian. She was already having doubts of her own, and feared he would weaken her already weakening resolve. However, he didn't say a word for over an hour—an hour during which she pushed him out of her mind every time he crept in. But his silence wore her down as persistent entreaties never could have.

She forced herself to really look at him for the first time since she noticed him praying in the car. ''He continued to have these attacks throughout his life,'' she found herself saying. "You needn't worry quite this much. Tomorrow he'll be right as rain."

"Then tomorrow I'll relax. You must have been scared out of your mind that first time, when he was so little. I'm sorry I wasn't home."

She didn't need his apology. It was years too late, and she'd forgiven him. Before she could tell him though, he jumped up like a jack-in-the-box, and stalked across the room to the windows, then paced back to his chair. He stayed seated for all of five seconds, before jumping back up again. "How much longer do we have to wait to hear how he is?"

"They'll come tell me when his breathing has stabilized," she told him, and hated the fear that flared in his gaze.

"Then he's been that way all this time? What's taking so long?"

"They give him inhalation therapy. It frees up his breathing. Sometimes it takes a long time," she explained, but added to herself as she wrung her hands that it had never taken this long before.

Jim raked his fingers through his hair. "Then why didn't they let you go with him?"

The man was a nervous wreck. "Do you always come this unglued in a crisis?"

He threw himself back into his chair. "Yes, as a matter of fact, I do. Hospitals make me a little crazy. It probably comes from my sister dying on me in one. I've gotten better over the years, but only when I've needed to be with church members. Not family or close friends." He jumped up again.

Holly realized that she still knew nothing about Jim's family. He'd never talked about them past a flip description that he'd had a typical family with two-point-two children. From that she'd just filled in the blanks with what she knew from her limited knowledge of life in America. Had their marriage been a complete sham, or had she never really asked enough questions?

She shook her head. What did it matter now? Why was she holding a mental requiem for a long-dead marriage. It was because her emotions were all on the surface and chaotic. One minute she was angry that he was there, and the next grateful. And his pacing wasn't helping matters a bit.

"Why don't you try praying again? At least that kept you from pacing around like a caged tiger. You're making *me* nervous now," she complained.

"I'm sorry. I've never been in this situation." Jim sat back down.

Holly's nerves snapped. "And whose fault is that?"

Ian's doctor stalked into the room. He looked none too happy. "No wonder Ian's hysterical if this is the kind of behavior he's been seeing. Mrs. Dillon, this is the sixth attack this month."

Holly stood and stiffened her spine. "I'm aware of that, Doctor."

Jim looked up and asked, "Is that unusual?"

"Are you the father he's all agitated about?"

Jim stood now too. "I'm his father. Are you saying I caused him to get sick?"

"Not directly. No." The doctor put out his hand. "I'm Dr. Robert Snyder."

Jim shook Dr. Snyder's hand. "Jim Dillon."

"Since we've never met, let me explain my role in Ian's care," Dr. Snyder said. "I'm a pediatric pulmonary specialist. Because of the complications emotional upsets can cause in asthmatics, especially children, I also minored in psychology. This way I am able to treat the whole patient. Could you tell me a little about your relationship with your son?"

"It's been rather short. Ian and I found each other on the Internet last month. He's been so happy we did. How can our finding each other be responsible for these attacks? And, if it is, wouldn't that mean this is all my fault?"

"Of course it does," Holly barked, knowing she sounded like a shrew, but unable to stop herself. It had taken so much longer than usual to stabilize Ian, and Holly knew it was a bad sign. She couldn't strike at the disease, so she lashed out at Jim. "Until you answered that message of Ian's, you were a figment of his imagination, and he was a happy little boy!"

Jim's lips tightened, and his eyes shot sparks. She could see that passive facade of his cracking again. Good. He didn't look like such a saint with fire in his eyes. Unfortunately, he also looked terribly much more attractive this way.

"He was sending e-mail messages to strange men, trying to find his father. I'd say he was far from content *or* safe."

"Well, he wasn't having attacks the way he is

now," Holly told him. She saw him wince, but refused to feel sorry for him. He was still too charming by half. She didn't need to hand him another weapon to use against her better judgment.

"Is that true?" he asked the doctor. "Am I to blame?"

"Let's all sit down, step back from finger pointing, and self-recriminations. First, the air quality in New York isn't the greatest, especially this time of year. It doesn't get much worse than this, and Ian says he spent a great deal of time outside today."

"Ian took off to find his long-lost father," Holly felt duty bound to point out.

"If you hadn't forbidden Ian to see me, he might not have been out taking buses across town looking for me."

The doctor sighed and pulled off his surgical hat. "Folks, petty bickering is not going to help your son. He *is* upset about you, Jim. For some reason he thinks you've been arrested for kidnapping him, and he's blaming himself. For the short-term, I want you both to go in there and reassure him that he hasn't caused his father to go to jail. My second suggestion is for you two to find some way to get along in his presence from now on. He'll be staying overnight, which should give you time to clear the air without Ian being caught in the middle.

"Next, I suggest you find a way to get him out of the city at least until the weather and smog clear. He also needs more help than I can give him. There's a specialist I'd like him to see, but he isn't here in New

York. He's gotten FDA approval to conduct a complete study on a new kind of treatment. They are about to start clinical trials with kids like Ian. I think your son is a perfect candidate, and though this is technically experimental, it also shows great promise. Another plus is that this new generation of drugs has contraindications that are very low level.''

"That's sounds hopeful," Holly said. "Where is this specialist? I'll take a leave of absence, and we'll leave at once."

Dr. Snyder grabbed a prescription pad out of his lab coat pocket and scribbled a name and phone number. "Here's his number. Call. Make an appointment. Mention my name, and tell him I want Ian seen there as soon as possible."

Holly looked down at the pad, and her stomach dropped. Is this some kind of sign? she wondered, as she stared down at the phone number with what she was terribly afraid was a Philadelphia area code. Maybe she was wrong. "Is this in Philadelphia?"

The doctor nodded. "Children's Hospital. You couldn't ask for a better facility or a better chance for Ian to live a normal life than with Dr. Roberts. Is that a problem? You seemed willing to take a leave of absence."

"No. It's no problem," she replied, refusing to look at Jim until the doctor left. When she did, she didn't see a gloating expression, but a concerned one, and she relaxed a little.

"Is this going to be a financial problem?" he

asked. "I mean I don't draw much salary, but I have a little money put aside. It's yours."

"I have back holiday pay, but I appreciate the offer. I can always look for a position there depending on how long this program takes. I'll need to change my visa status, which shouldn't be too much of a problem. Ian's an American citizen, of course, so that's one less piece of red tape. Then I'll need to—"

Jim reached over and took her hand. "Holly. You're babbling. I'm sorry. I know you're uncomfortable with me showing up this way, and with having to bring him to my vicinity for treatment, but maybe it's the Lord's will."

She nodded. She really didn't like to consider that as a possibility, but she had little choice. Jim *had* shown up on the particular day when Ian had his most severe attack to date, then his doctor *had* decided to send Ian to be treated near where Jim lived. It really was all a bit too much to be a coincidence.

"Maybe it *is* the Lord," she said, trying to ignore the feel of Jim's hand on hers.

"I have friends who live a good way out of the city in Chester County. They attend the Tabernacle, that's my church. They have an apartment on the second floor of their carriage house that I'll bet they'd let you use. It's within commuting distance to Philadelphia by train or car, but the air's fresh and relatively free of pollution. It would be good for Ian, and they have a whole passel of kids around his age, so he'd have playmates. Would you like me to call and see if they'd let you stay there?"

Holly shook her head. It was happening too fast. Her hasty marriage to Jim Dillon had cured Holly for good of rushing in where angels fear to tread. "I don't know. I need time. You can ask, but I'd insist on paying rent. And my answer isn't necessarily yes. I'll have to think about it, and give you my answer in the morning. We could commute from here as well, after all."

Holly stared into her bathroom mirror later that night, and wondered what she had been thinking by telling Jim that she'd consider his idea. She should have just said no. She hadn't really intended to even consider the ludicrous idea until she'd gone in to see Ian after Jim left.

Her son's eyes had been shining, and she'd instantly thought Jim had mentioned Philadelphia and Children's Hospital. But he hadn't. Ian had just been happy and grateful to her for having made sure Jim was safe and sound from the policemen. And his over-the-top gratitude had her terribly worried.

If she continued to keep them apart, would Ian look at her with hate rather than love shining in his eyes? And if that didn't happen now wouldn't it happen later? She'd seen it often enough. Small acts of defiance like today's trek across the city could turn to bigger more dangerous exploits as he grew older. It was a possibility and even thinking about it was frightening.

She had to tread carefully and think about her options. There was no question that Ian would benefit from the Philadelphia program, and seeing more of Jim at the same time would also benefit her son's health, and his attitude. He was clearly obsessed with his father. That Jim would hurt Ian eventually was a great possibility, but if her son remained as close as ever to her, she could help him through his disappointment.

Holly now knew the true meaning of being caught between a rock and a hard place. She got a sinking feeling in her stomach. There was only one solution to the whole mess. It wasn't perfect, but it was a solution. She would have to let Ian spend this time near Jim, but she would be there to protect him physically the way she hadn't been for her brother and sister. And she'd be there to pick up the pieces of her son's shattered heart if Jim had not changed as much as he said.

But she would keep herself as emotionally distant from Jim Dillon as possible, because if she'd learned one thing during the hours she'd been with him that day, it was that she was just as susceptible to him as she had been years ago. She'd wanted to comfort him. Wanted to believe him. Wanted his touch. And she would never fall into that trap again. Some lessons in life were just too painful to have to relearn.

Chapter Three

Jim walked into the pediatric waiting room the next morning. It was where he'd last seen Holly, but either she hadn't yet arrived, or she was already in with Ian. He still couldn't believe how badly their reunion had gone. It had been the complete opposite of any dream he'd ever had of meeting Holly again. Of course, dreams usually had little to do with reality or the self-made disasters of the past. His had been no exception.

But even in his wildest nightmares he hadn't been introduced into Holly's life again while handcuffed by New York's finest and accused of kidnapping their son. Thank the Lord he'd taken Harry up on his offer of a ride to Holly's, or Jim had a feeling he'd have wound up spending the night at the city's expense. It was only through Harry's intervention that the cop had taken him up to Holly's apartment and not straight to the station house.

He thought of her reaction to seeing him again. Jim pursed his lips and shook his head. The truth hurt, but he had to face it. Holly hated him. There was no question of that. He deserved it, he knew. But it still hurt. He'd hoped she would at the very least see him as a changed man. A man changed by Jesus. And he'd thought that maybe she would respect him for how far he'd come from the gutter he'd ended up in. But he knew that he didn't always get what he wanted.

As long as he got what he needed—contact with his son—then he'd be grateful, Jim told himself.

The elevator opened and he watched Holly step through the doors. Her dark-auburn hair fell loosely about her shoulders. Shoulders that slumped just a bit as she walked down the hall. She drew closer and he could see dark smudges beneath her green eyes that told him she'd spent a sleepless night. He wondered if worry over Ian had kept her awake or if it was Dr. Snyder's suggestion of the Children's Hospital program that had cost her sleep.

Looking at the situation from her point of view, why should she take his word that he had his life together and that he had been sober for more than six years? He had promised over and over not to drink again during their marriage.

But he always had.

Jim knew from experience that it was difficult to believe the changes that God could cause in someone's life. He hadn't believed it himself until he'd gotten more than a free meal at a neighborhood mission one hot summer night. But from what Ian had said, Holly shared Jim's beliefs and took Ian to church. So why did she find it so hard to believe the Lord had changed him?

Jim watched Holly tense even more when she spotted him and felt a pang in the region of his heart. It was so hard to abandon all hope, when he wanted to earn not only her respect, but her love again, as well. He knew there was no other woman on earth who could complete his life the way Holly could. But she hated him and distrusted him even more.

He stood as she drew closer and tried to cover his reaction to the exhaustion she couldn't hide. What hurt the most was that he knew it was his fault that she looked as if she'd been dragged backward through a keyhole. He loved her. He didn't want to hurt her. If this were any other situation, he would bow out and disappear the way he had before. But this was an issue he couldn't abandon. It wasn't only about him and Holly. He had a moral duty and a clawing need inside him to be a father to Ian. He knew all too well what it felt like growing up knowing his father had abandoned him. Jim just couldn't let Ian think he didn't care.

"Holly, could we talk?" he asked and gestured to the chair near where he'd been sitting. "I know you said you'd give me your decision this morning, but before you do, there's something I wanted to say that I didn't get a chance to say yesterday."

"I won't be talking to you that long so I don't need to sit. And there's certainly no need to plead your case. I know what you want."

"No, I don't think you do," he replied, trying not to let her see that he wanted her in his life as much as he wanted a relationship with Ian. "But that isn't the issue here. Right now all I want is to apologize. For the man I was. For the husband I wasn't. For the disappointment that I made of our marriage. I want to promise you, one last time, that I will never drink again. And most of all, I want to assure you that I won't ever hurt you or Ian again."

Jim saw anger enter Holly's expression before she masked it. Why would his apology make her angry?

"I forgave you long ago. I had to so I could go on. Forgiving you let me get past it. I've decided to take you up on your offer, if your friends don't mind my renting their apartment. I've already gotten the ball rolling with Ian's records. As for your promise not to hurt us, we'll see.

"But understand, you and I will never be friends, Jim. We're Ian's parents. I'll give you a chance to be a father to him and hide my feelings. For his sake only. And for his sake, we'll be polite with each other but that's all."

Jim nodded. "I understand." It wasn't the kind of relationship he'd dreamed of, but he understood her feelings better than she could know.

"Furthermore," she continued, her stance a bit more militant, "I warn you, if you mess up, you won't get a second chance. I won't see my son in a box as I did my brother and sister. I'll be out of the U.S. and Ian will be out of your reach faster than you can blink if I ever get wind of you touching a drop of alcohol. Got it?''

He nodded again, though he could have told her it would never come to that. Her threat was of little consequence, because with God's help, he'd be a good father. It hurt just as much though, because he deserved her mistrust. ''Can I tell him about you two coming to Pennsylvania or can I at least be there when you do?''

''We'll tell him together when I get back from settling with the cashier.''

Jim watched as she walked away, tension in every line of her body. He told himself that he'd never really thought she had truly forgiven him as she'd said, so it didn't matter that she'd essentially thrown his apology in his face. But it did. It mattered a lot. She didn't seem to want to spend one more minute in his company than she had to. He wondered if she had any idea how much it hurt him to spend time with the woman he would love until he drew his last breath, knowing she hated the very sight of him.

Be thankful for Ian, he told himself. Ian's love in his life would be enough. It had to be.

Jim peeked around the door to the playroom where the nurse on duty told him he'd find his son. And there he was, building with those colorful little connecting blocks Jim was always picking up around the church. But he had to admit that he'd never seen a boy Ian's age put together such an elaborate structure before.

"Hi, Ian," he called as he entered. "Ready to head out of here?"

"G'day, Dad," Ian said in that international accent of his. It had confused Jim until Ian had explained that Holly had been stationed in London where her current boss had been ambassador. She had apparently met Anders when he hired her while she was living in Australia. Which explained why Jim had been unable to find her in New Zealand. And it also explained why Ian's accent was such a curious mix of Kiwi, Australian, British and New York. Holly had certainly become a world traveler and Ian right along with her.

"Actually, I'm having quite a good time," Ian told him. "I've never had so many of these to work with before. I'm designing an addition to the United Nations Building. It's rather boxy looking the way it is. Don't you think?"

Jim tilted his head to one side, considering the bright-blue-red-and-yellow structure. He could just make out the shape of the world-famous building within his son's design. Jim chuckled. "You know, Ian, you're right. Yours does have more character. But then, I don't think there's enough land to do this. Keep it in mind, though. You never know what the future may bring."

"Redesigning the UN again? And in 3-D this time!" Holly called out as she breezed into the room and bent to hug Ian. She had such a sweet smile on her face and such pride in her eyes as she looked at their son. Ian was one lucky little boy to have Holly for a mother. Jim wished just once she'd look at him that way again.

He looked up at her and their gazes caught and held for a moment more than was comfortable. Then a look of anger came into her eyes and Jim looked away.

"Is—is everything all right?" Ian asked, worry evident in his voice.

"Poppet, what could be wrong?" she asked Ian.

"Well, you were awfully angry with Dad last night."

"I was terribly anxious about *you*. You mustn't ever do anything like that again."

Ian blushed a bit. "I know. Dad's already told me that when he was bringing me home. I'm sorry. I won't do it again. I promise."

"That's good because now we have this problem. I mean, here we all are just sitting around in a hospital waiting for them to come with the wheelchair so you can leave. It's really holding up our plans. We have a lot of packing to do in the next few days."

"Plans? What sort of plans?" Ian asked.

"Maybe we should tell him about those plans now," Jim urged.

Holly ignored him, but smiled at Ian. "Dr. Snyder wants you to get out of the city for a while, and see a new doctor, who's discovered a new treatment program for your kind of asthma. And it just so happens that it is in Philadelphia."

"You mean it, Mum? I get to go live with Dad?"

Holly reared back as if Ian had hit her. She looked

absolutely stricken, and Jim couldn't blame her. She'd raised Ian all these years and here he steps up to the plate and hits a home run with the kid.

"Not quite, Son," Jim said. "I'd love to have you, but my apartment is really just two rooms. One to sleep in and one to sit, eat and read in. I even use the church kitchen to cook. Your mother is coming to Philadelphia, too. Friends of mine have an apartment you two will live in while you're in the program. I won't be far away, but you'll still live with your Mum. And the best part is, they have kids around your age and a huge piece of property where you can run and play."

"Wow. That sounds super, Dad. When do we go, Mum?"

A rattle at the door drew Jim's attention. "Here's your transportation out of here, Son," he said then he turned to Holly. "How are you planning to get there? Do you have a car? Should I write down directions for you?"

Holly took a deep breath. "I appreciate the concern but I've been on my own for years now. I'm sure we'll be just fine. I *would* like the phone number for these people, so I can make arrangements with them."

"Well, sure. If that's how you want to do it." He took out one of his business cards and wrote down the number. "Here's Maggie and Trent's number, and mine's on the flip side in case you need anything. I'm headed home from here. I'll be back there by this afternoon if you want to e-mail me about anything. When do you think you'll arrive?''

"Ian's evaluation is scheduled for Monday. I wouldn't count on us much before sometime late Sunday. It will take me that long to pack and clear up some things with the ambassador.''

Jim squatted down in front of Ian's wheelchair and smiled at his son. "You take care now and I'll see you soon.'' He stood and stared down at Holly who had a slightly glazed look in her eyes as she stared back at him. He wished she'd slept better. "Have a good night's sleep and drive carefully when you head down my way.''

A wonderful terrifying urge to kiss her nearly overcame all his reason, so Jim quickly leaned down and gave Ian a peck on the cheek instead. He noticed she jumped backward a step as he bent past her toward Ian. "See you both soon,'' he said then turned to leave mother and son alone.

He took one last look over his shoulder and noticed them both watching him. Ian's face wore a look of love so apparent that he felt warmed to his core, but not so Holly. He wouldn't call what he saw in her eyes fury this time, either. He'd actually have preferred that. Because what he saw stabbed at his heart so viciously that he had to draw a sharp breath to make himself breathe again. Holly. His precious Holly looked for all the world as if she feared him.

Fix it, Lord. Please. Somehow. Some way. Please give me a chance to show her that I'd never hurt her or Ian again. That's not all that much to ask, is it, Lord?

* * *

Holly tiptoed into Ian's room and found him asleep, but his computer was still up in the mail program where he composed and read all his messages. Drawn like a fly to honey she walked to his desk and sat. There were several messages for her that she'd never read. Messages from Jim. She decided to read the first to see what he'd said.

Half an hour later she closed and deleted the last one. He seemed so changed. Not that he had ever been violent or even particularly nasty. He'd been the kind of drunk who was quiet but who wanted to be around people. In those circumstances, he laughed at jokes his friends told, but when he was alone, he'd sit and stare into space, unreachable and unapproachable. He'd had a flat way of staring at her when she'd gotten angry and shouted. It had said that his heart was as empty as the expression in his eyes.

The man who wrote the messages she'd just read had a quiet spiritual strength she found hard to ignore. His first message had been a carefully worded request for permission to write to Ian. She'd given Ian her verbal okay and so her permission had gone to Jim by way of Ian. In the second, he praised her for the wonderful child she'd raised and asked for an address so he could begin sending support payments. The third had expressed his joy and thanks, because, from some of the things Ian wrote, Jim could tell they attended church. And again he'd asked for her address.

He'd sent another message tonight. Again he'd praised her for the son she'd raised, and he'd thanked her for letting him be a part of Ian's life. There was a brief history about the people who owned the carriage house where she and Ian would stay while Ian was in treatment.

Trent and Maggie Osborne were raising their nieces and nephews, who had been orphaned when Trent's brother and his wife were killed in a traffic mishap. He'd ended with another apology for his failures in the past.

Jim just didn't seem to realize that the worst offense he'd committed against her was that he'd chosen liquor over their marriage. When she'd asked for a divorce that morning, he'd become angry, true, but he hadn't even tried to change her mind. He'd just left her with a haunting parting shot, and had walked out of her life and the life of his son.

How could a man rejoice in her salvation and not realize how badly his easy-come-easy-go attitude toward the end of their marriage had hurt her?

Men! They were all idiots!

Chapter Four

Holly looked away from the ribbon of asphalt that twisted and turned ahead of her to the directions the Osbornes had given her. This was the proper road, all right, but it seemed endless. It was hard to believe there could be an area so rural only an hour and a half outside a city as large as Philadelphia.

Glancing quickly in her rearview mirror, Holly saw Ian once again pouring over the stack of information on the area that he'd pulled off the Web last night, while she'd finished packing. His enthusiasm worried her, because she was afraid he was in for a huge disappointment. Not in Pennsylvania but in his father.

"Did you know Dad grew up in Pittsburgh before he went into the navy?"

"Actually, I didn't," she answered truthfully. That was one of the many things about Jim she had never learned. Just being on the arm of the tall, attentive sailor had been so exciting that until it was too late she hadn't noticed his reluctance to talk about his life prior to joining the navy. Now that she thought about it, she didn't even know how old he'd been when he'd asked her to marry him, so she had no idea how old he was even now.

She supposed his age had been on their marriage license, but she'd never really read the piece of paper that had linked her legally to her handsome young husband. Before the wedding ceremony it had been one more bit of red tape keeping them apart; then after they'd separated she'd convinced herself that she no longer cared.

Suddenly she did care. And that bothered her. A lot!

Ian's deep theatrical sigh brought her back to the present. "He's just so grand, Mum. I don't know why you didn't stay married to him."

"I've explained about that," she said with forced calm, trying hard not to sound snappish.

"But you were just being kind with your answers. I know all about the wrong things he did."

Holly was horrified. How much had Ian overheard the other day? A psychologist she'd consulted a few years ago had warned her not to speak ill of Ian's absent father when he asked questions, because children found their sense of identity in both their parents. So she'd guarded her words and explanations about the divorce and the reasons for it.

"Those things were between your father and me," she said carefully, hoping to prolong his innocence as long as possible. She didn't want Jim on a pedestal because she knew he'd eventually fall off, but neither did she want him in the gutter destroying Ian's sense of himself.

"You had nothing whatever to do with what happened between us," she added. "You must forget the things you heard me say to him the other night. I was terribly angry when I thought he'd talked you into seeing him against my wishes."

"I only heard loud voices that night, Mum," Ian explained in that half-adult, patient way of his. "I heard that he drank too much from *him*. He told the people in the church about how he lost us and how sorry he is about his sins. He's new because of Jesus, he said. But he looked like he was crying while telling about it all, so I guess Jesus didn't take away the hurt. I just think perhaps you should have waited for Jesus to change him."

Holly could scarcely breathe, so sharp was the dagger her son's innocent words sent into her heart. She tried to ignore the old voice that had haunted her so often over the years but couldn't. *He should have loved you enough to quit drinking for your sake.*

But this time another voice intruded. It was Jim's voice and the last words he'd spoken to her eight years ago, after she'd told him their marriage was over. "You put me on a pedestal and hated me when I fell off. I didn't ask to be there, Holly. You decided who I was, and now that you know I'm just me, you don't want me anymore. At least it was you I fell in love with. Who did you fall in love with, anyway?"

It seemed that once again Jim had been unable to keep someone who loved him from placing him high above other mere mortals. But it was no longer her job to worry about Jim, she told herself. *Ian* was her concern. She could only hope that, if Jim toppled off this new pedestal Ian had placed him on, her son wouldn't be hurt as deeply by it as she had been. She vowed to watch closely so she'd be there if it happened. *When* it happens, she corrected cynically.

And she'd be there to keep Ian safe. She would never abandon him the way her father had her. That had been the worst part of her mother's drinking. Reverend Willis had been so determined to deny what was happening, and to pretend all was well that he failed his children. She would not fail Ian in the same way.

"There, Mum! Look, we've almost arrived. See the sign? Two more miles."

Holly breathed a sigh. Finally this endless anticipation would be over. "It certainly became rural as we traveled. Won't it be lovely not to be in crowds for a while?"

Ian fidgeted in his seat. "Oh, yes. I don't really like New York, you know. It would be so pleasant if the children Dad talked about could be my mates. I'd be able to go see them without being taken to their door the way you and Nanny have to in New York."

Holly felt a little pang. He didn't like New York? How had she missed that? she wondered, making a mental note to take him out of the city more often.

She watched for road signs more carefully now,

and made several turns on to twisting roads that rose and fell with the rolling terrain. All along the roads were fences. White ones that gleamed in the strong sunlight and silvery split rail types that blended with nature. Finally they came to a sign at the roadside. Small flowers were painted in a looping vine that spelled out Paradise Found, and under that was a set of three numbers.

Holly slowed to a stop and gazed up the long drive at a large Victorian house that sat atop a hill. It was like something out of a turn-of-the-century history book. Painted a creamy taupe except for the window sashes that were deep barn red and some miscellaneous trim done in a crisp forest green, it seemed to call welcome. Behind her Ian laughed.

"Mum, look at the house. Doesn't it look as if it's looking down at us?"

She chuckled and silently thanked Paradise Found for easing some of her mounting tension. "Those are called eyebrow windows. Houses like this often had them cut into the roofs. It's meant to add a bit of whimsy, and I'd say it succeeded."

"What kind of wood is the roof made of?"

"I believe those are cedar shakes much like we saw in England. I'd say Mr. Osborne spared no expense on his house. Let's hope our apartment is as well renovated. This house is nearly a hundred years old, and Mrs. Osborne said the carriage house is just as old. That's quite old for a house in the States."

Just then a tall man stepped out onto the porch. He was followed by Jim. And Holly's heart started to pound. Why did he have to be so handsome? So compelling? Why did she always have to feel this way at first sight of him?

Her tension was back a hundredfold. *This is a huge mistake!* Holly wanted with all her heart to drive on by and call Jim to say she and Ian would be staying elsewhere.

Then Ian put the window down and shouted, "Dad! We've arrived!"

Guilt assailed her. They were staying here for Ian's sake. Not hers. What was the matter with her?

She pressed her foot to the accelerator, drove as far as the house, and put the car in park. Her hands fairly shook. Then just as she returned the rear window to a closed position, Ian sprang from the car, and ran to his father. She had no choice but to follow. As she stepped from the car, Jim loped down the steps off the front porch, a broad smile on his handsome face.

Life just isn't fair. People should be as ugly as the lives they've led as a forewarning to the rest of us.

She watched as Ian barreled up to Jim who caught him in a bear hug before turning to his friend who approached them. She assumed he must be Trent Osborne, and was surprised that the two men were like bookends. Equal in height, dark good looks and killer smiles.

Laughing, Jim turned away from the man and walked to her, Ian still in his arms. Ian looked so small and vulnerable suddenly that her chest tightened. This man could destroy her son's life.

Yours, too, that doom-and-gloom voice inside her warned.

Holly suddenly recalled the way her heart had speeded up in the hospital playroom, when she'd stared into Jim's hazel eyes, and had seen things he had no right to want of her. She'd been furious with him, and truthfully with herself, for the flash of a second, when she wanted the same things he did. Then he'd bent toward Ian to kiss him, and for a scary, split second she'd thought he'd meant to kiss her. She forced herself to be honest about that fear. It wasn't fear of Jim, but fear of her own yearning for that kiss that had frightened her.

Still frightened her.

She could never survive a repeat of her disastrous marriage. It wasn't a physical fear but an emotional one. Sober or drunk Jim had never been violent. His low-key personality had been a breath of fresh air to a girl brought up in a house full of tension from the need to protect the family secret.

But the drinking, which she'd brushed aside when her father had pointed it out in Jim, had turned her husband into a monster in the months following their marriage. Low-key had quickly become brooding and uncommunicative. It was a silence that had consumed every ounce of her energy and her love for her young husband.

Holly forced her suddenly shaking legs toward the front of the car. She stood and watched all three approach. "I see you found us all right. Did you make good time?" Jim called casually. His eyes were bright and clear. He seemed so different from the man he'd been. Could Jesus have changed him as much as those e-mail messages indicated?

"Make good time?" Holly asked, wondering if she'd missed anything with her musings.

Jim laughed then explained, "That means that it didn't take you too long to drive down here. You didn't get into much traffic."

Holly chuckled at her misunderstanding of certain American idioms even after two years in the country. "The only traffic we encountered was in the cities. Although for a while I thought we were lost. It feels so isolated here."

"I would have been happy to come up and bring you both down."

Stop being so nice, she wanted to shout, and fought to keep her expression neutral while sternly warning herself not to put her faith in him again. It could all be a trick. Smoke and mirrors. And it was her job to watch from the sidelines and protect Ian and, at all costs, not to get caught up in the lies all over again.

"You're in the middle of horse country, Mrs. Dillon," Trent Osborne said as Jim swung Ian to the ground.

"Holly. Please. We're about to become neighbors, after all."

Trent inclined his head in agreement. "Holly, then. Welcome to Paradise Found. And you too, Ian."

"What's that mean? Paradise Found?" her son asked.

A shadow seemed to pass across Trent Osborne's

face. "My brother and his wife named it, so I don't know for sure. To my wife Maggie and me, it means that we found a little corner of paradise right here. I hope you do, too."

"Why don't you just ask him?" Ian asked, squinting against the bright sunlight as he looked up at the man.

Holly wanted to slink from sight, knowing the tragic answer to her son's inquiry. "Ian, it's very rude to question adults."

Trent smiled sadly. "It's okay. I'm pretty used to kids and their questions," he told Holly, then turned his attention to Ian. "I can't ask them, son. My brother and his wife died in a car accident a couple of years ago."

Ian's little brow wrinkled. "Oh, that's too bad. My grandmother and aunt and uncle died in a car smack-up, as well. I was just born, so I didn't know them, but it makes Mum sad still."

Trent went down on one knee and put his hand on Ian's shoulder. Holly wondered if this was how Jim had learned to speak to children from their own level. "I still miss him, but I know he and his wife are happy in heaven, and that they know they gave me the greatest gift I could ever get. See, they had children who became my children. And having them in my life made me see that I needed God in my life, as well."

"When can I meet them?" Ian asked.

"They're at their grandmother's house, but they should be home soon." He turned his head and stood at the sound of a car and smiled. "Actually, you're about to meet them now."

"Suppose I get Holly settled in while you introduce the kids," Jim said to his friend.

"Good idea. You need to drive around back. There's a spot next to the carriage house for your car," Trent said as Jim moved to the passenger door of her car. "Jim helped me renovate the place so he can show you around the apartment just as well as Maggie or I can. Come over to meet my wife when you have a minute. Okay?"

Holly nodded and pasted on a smile. What besides yes could she say with Ian looking on, excited to meet his future mates? It was just as well. This way, out of Ian's hearing, she could set some ground rules with Jim. The first and last of which were that the only connection between them was Ian. "That should do just fine. Jim and I have some things to settle."

She got into the car without another word, and sucked in a sharp breath when Jim's wide shoulder brushed hers. "Sorry," he muttered looking decidedly uncomfortable in the small auto.

Not liking the closeness, either, but more than likely for an entirely different reason, Holly drove quickly around to the back of the house. Jim said nothing, thank goodness, and soon she threw open her door and scrambled out. She watched Jim unfold himself from the subcompact, then tossed him the keys as soon as he was upright. "The luggage is in the boot. Is the door to the apartment locked?"

Jim's eyes sparked. She could see him wrestle with

his anger for a few seconds before getting hold of it. He took a deep breath and nodded. "Go ahead and explore. I'll be along," he said then turned away.

And Holly felt about as tall as an ant. Disgusted with herself for treating him like a servant, and not even sure why she had done so, she went up the steps and into the apartment. She froze in utter awe just inside the door. It was a perfect little dollhouse. There were a great abundance of windows that sparkled in the afternoon light, and when combined with a warm cream color on the textured walls, the room was downright cheery. There was a comfortable-looking burgundy-colored, camel-backed sofa facing a stone fireplace and an equally inviting overstuffed chair off to the side angled toward the sofa. The kitchen stood to the left on the other side of an island that separated it from the living room area.

She walked to the fireplace, and stared up at a landscape by an artist who recently had made a grand splash in her first showing in New York. The Osbornes had certainly spared no expense in fixing up this little apartment. She'd never been able to afford to live anywhere quite so lovely.

"Do you remember David Chernak?" Jim asked as he thumped down several suitcases just inside the door.

"Your friend in the navy who sounded so different from you. He was from the South, wasn't it?"

"Yeah. That was him."

"We had dinner at their house a time or two. His wife Regina was a timid little American who hardly ever spoke no matter how hard I tried to get to know her.''

"They're divorced and he's married to someone else, now. It was Cassidy who painted that for me as a thank-you for conducting their marriage ceremony. My place is too small for it, so Maggie hung it up here to keep it safe for me.''

Holly frowned. She'd been so envious of Regina because David had been clearly so besotted with her. "But he adored her. Wasn't the marriage a conflict for you because of his divorce?"

Jim shook his head. "He's had a lot of upheaval in his life, and losing her was just the beginning. I'll tell you about it sometime if you're interested in a long story. But right now I got the idea you wanted to talk to me about something."

What was the matter with her—carrying on a conversation with him about old times as if the two of them were on friendly terms! How did he draw her in this way? Holly stood a little straighter. "Actually, I thought we needed to get a few ground rules straight between us," she said a bit too sharply.

That sizzle instantly flared in Jim's gaze once again. "Ground rules? Holly, you're here for Ian to see a specialist. I know you aren't here in any way, shape or form for my sake. I want to spend more time with Ian, but don't worry, I don't intend to inflict myself on you. You've made your feelings toward me abundantly clear. You can't stand the sight of me. I've got it! Okay? You don't need to beat it into my head.''

Holly felt her cheeks heat. Was that the way she seemed to him? "I—I just thought—"

"That I was here today because of you," he finished for her. "Wrong. I was here for lunch and to help Trent with something. I was about to leave when you arrived. I'm sorry Trent suggested I show you around. Maggie isn't feeling well and he wanted to go back in and check on her. Now, if you'll excuse me, I have to go home and finish my lesson for tonight. I was going to suggest we go to the hospital tomorrow together, since I know where it is, but I wouldn't consider bothering you. I'll be there at eight-thirty. If that's a problem, then say so now when Ian's not here."

"It's not a problem."

"Good. There are a few more small bags in the car. I'm sure you'd prefer to get them yourself."

Jim pivoted and stomped down the steps toward his pickup. Did she think he was completely dense? Did she think he hadn't gotten the message loud and clear at the hospital how much she hated him? Or how she couldn't stand to be within fifty feet of him?

Well, he wasn't stupid, and he wasn't a masochist either! If she didn't want him around, he'd make sure he wasn't. She could send Ian over to Trent and Maggie's, and he'd pick him up there when they had their visits.

His mind in a turmoil, Jim drove home, and by the time he got there, his anger had left him. But without the buffer of anger, he was left alone, and feeling battered. He slid down in the front seat of his aging pickup and stared up at the barn he'd lovingly restored to house the church. The Tabernacle.

Tears blurred his vision and he prayed for patience and peace. He closed his eyes and Holly's face filled his mind the same way his love for her filled his heart. And so he prayed for a miracle, but he held out little hope it would be granted. He was only reaping what he'd sown years ago. It had been his drinking that had destroyed Holly's love and turned it to hate, after all.

"I shouldn't have asked for more." Jim spoke aloud, as he often did when asking for the Lord's help. "I'm sorry. It's just that I know I would be a good husband for her now, and I'd be so complete with her by my side. But You've given me back a chance with Ian." He sighed, and went slack against the seat. "He's enough, Lord. You're enough. Please, help me to rest in You, and to be content with all You've given me."

Chapter Five

❧

Jim pulled into a spot in the high-rise parking garage across the street from Children's Hospital the next morning. He checked his watch and breathed a sigh of relief. After oversleeping, he'd had to make a mad dash to get ready and still he'd been running late. But then traffic had been a dream and he'd made the trip into the city with ten minutes to spare. And some people didn't believe in miracles anymore, he thought with a grin.

He's been running late, because he'd overslept thanks to a mostly sleepless night. After tossing and turning for a couple of hours, he'd given up on sleep and had turned to prayer about his relationship with Holly. No answers had come to him, however. He shrugged and jumped out of the truck. The answer would occur to him eventually. A wise old woman he'd met once had said that time would tell its answers only when it was ready.

Time would tell. The thought halted Jim in his tracks. He gazed unseeingly out over the rooftops of the University City section of Center City, Philadelphia. Maybe that was his answer. All night he'd asked God the same question in a hundred different ways. Would Holly ever see the changes the Lord had brought about in him? The question had haunted him because he knew that if he continued to treat her the way he had when they parted yesterday, she surely never would.

Hands in his back pockets, he closed his eyes and took a deep breath. He was once again in a place that the Lord always seemed to take him. It was a place that made him see the futility of putting his own fingers into the pie. It was a place where he learned once again to let God guide his life.

How many times had he told his congregation the same thing? He chuckled at his own foolishness. Sometimes, he thought, *Let God* was a Christian's hardest lesson to learn even though in the long run it was the easiest cure for problems anyone would ever find.

Let God soften hearts. *Let God* show the way. *Let God* intervene in situations.

Jim admitted that he might teach the lesson often, but it was clear that he himself hadn't mastered it quite yet, either. He shook his head and grinned ruefully. *All right, Lord. Do Your stuff. Tell me what to say. Tell me when to shut up. And most important, tell me when to do just plain nothing.*

It took five minutes for him to reach the office of

Dr. Wilson Roberts and a couple more for Holly and Ian to arrive. As they entered Ian waved and called, "G'day, Dad." Then he ran toward Jim, his arms reaching out. Jim's eyes misted as he lifted Ian high into the air, holding his son securely. Jim had missed so many hugs in eight years that every one was infinitely precious to him.

As Ian wrapped his arms around Jim's neck, he noticed that there were circles under Holly's eyes. She looked tired and drawn. "Let's all sit down," he suggested.

"I imagine I have quite a bit of information to fill out," Holly said. "Ian, why don't you chat up your father while I see about giving the nurse your medical history."

"Right-o," Ian said, an obvious veteran of doctors' offices. It was still hard for Jim to look at his tall healthy-looking son as a boy with a serious medical problem.

When Holly returned and began filling in the blanks on the form, he watched her with growing unease. He'd known that he'd missed good times but as the seconds turned to minutes and she wrote line after line in her neat script, the raft of papers came to represent something Jim hadn't really thought much about during those years of searching.

The bad times.

And apparently there had been a lot of bad times.

Bored, Ian ventured over to a play area of the large waiting room that was clearly designed more for the pint-size patients than for their parents. Jim fished out his insurance card from his pocket and handed it to Holly. "I added Ian to my medical insurance." He handed her the card. "Could I see the forms before you give them to the nurse? I should have some idea of his medical history."

Her expression grave, Holly nodded and finished the line she'd been working on. After filling in the information from his medical card, she handed it back. When she gave him the forms a moment later, she looked at him as if she were sizing up a stranger. Confused, he looked away and started reading Ian's medical history.

"I'm so sorry," he whispered to her minutes later.

Holly looked up at him, perplexed.

"I may have been looking for him and been frustrated all these years by our separation, but you've had so much to deal with day in and day out," he explained. "You've dealt with so much worry and fear, and you were all alone."

For once, Holly did not try to tear his head off and hand it to him. She shook her head. "Jim, I haven't been alone. I rediscovered my faith in the Lord shortly after I moved to Australia. He's been my strong tower and Ian's."

Jim smiled sadly. "I'm glad He was there when I couldn't be but I *am* here now. Let me help. Please. I can at least do that much, can't I?"

Holly bit her lip and nodded. "I'm sorry about yesterday. I guess it was pretty conceited to assume you were at the Osbornes to see *me*. They're your friends, after all. And, Ian was arriving. I was probably the last person you wanted to see, as well.''

Jim nearly winced, hearing what she hadn't said outright. He'd been the last person *she'd* wanted to see. He didn't share her feelings. Should he tell her exactly how glad he'd been that she'd arrived when he'd still been there? No. He'd only been thinking about his feelings for her, when Ian was in the hospital in New York, and Holly had somehow known and had looked at him with fury in her eyes. She could barely tolerate his presence.

God had spoken to him in the garage and he had to heed His counsel. Any change in Holly's feelings for him would come slowly and would have to come from the Lord. They wouldn't come about through Jim's own feeble efforts, that was for sure. But neither could he lie to Holly about his feelings for her. A lie would never honor God and that was what Jim's life was all about.

''I wasn't there to see you, but I certainly didn't mind that you arrived while I was still there,'' Jim told her quietly. ''I'll always care about you. You were my wife and *are* the mother of my son.''

Holly had no time to react, because the nurse called out through her reception window. ''Mrs. Dillon. Ian. The doctor is ready for you.''

''Isn't Dad coming in with us?'' Ian asked, as he jumped up from the floor.

Jim, who'd stood automatically, almost said, ''Of course I am,'' but instead from somewhere deep inside where obedience to the Lord overruled pride came a wholly different reply. "I'd like to, if that's okay with you, Holly?"

Holly stared at him for a few moments then nodded. Holding Ian's hand as they walked down the wide corridor, waiting for the results of tests and then listening to the doctor's decision changed him forever. For the first time, he was a father.

Hours later, as he walked Ian and Holly to her little subcompact, Jim was a *grateful* father. Dr. Roberts had indeed accepted Ian into his experimental program.

The doctor planned to treat not only the symptoms but also to attack the cause of Ian's asthma. They would be giving Ian something called anti-IgE antibodies. The hope was that he would have fewer attacks and be able to stop using the steroids that caused him severe side effects. If it worked, the drug would be submitted for FDA approval and millions would benefit.

It made both him and Holly a little nervous to think of Ian being used as what amounted to a human guinea pig, but it was their son's best chance to live a normal life without a heaven-sent miracle cure.

Jim still intended to pray for his son's complete healing but he also acknowledged that sometimes God uses men to do His bidding and that doctors might rank among the men most often used.

"Would you like to go somewhere to grab a bite to eat?" Jim found himself asking Holly quietly. Ian ran ahead to press a plate on the wall that opened a big set of double doors leading to the parking garage.

"Or maybe we could take Ian to see some of the historical sights in Old City."

Holly stopped and turned to him. "I don't know if that's a good idea."

Jim shrugged, trying not to show his disappointment. "I just thought it might give me a little time with Ian. Sort of a supervised visit. We'd be in public places. I hoped you'd feel more comfortable about him being with me that way. I don't know how else to start spending time with him that would still let you see that he's safe with me."

"I hadn't thought that far ahead," she admitted.

"Well, hey, I certainly understand your reluctance. I don't want to force you to spend time in my company. Forget it. I guess I could come over and toss a ball around with him in Trent and Maggie's yard or something like that." He shrugged again, carelessly he hoped, and walked toward Ian who was dancing around in the open doorway.

"Are the Liberty Bell and Independence Hall in this Old City?" she asked.

Jim looked back. Holly wasn't smiling but she didn't look angry, either. Just uncertain. He nodded. "And Betsy Ross House is nearby. Tradition says that's where she made our first flag. We could eat at City Tavern and Ian would probably like The Marine Corp Museum and Carpenters Hall. If there's time, the U.S. Mint does demonstrations on coin minting, too."

"I suppose it might be good for Ian to see some

of his heritage. I imagine you consider America to be a large part of his heritage.''

Jim blinked. He hadn't thought of that at all. A little ashamed for taking the kind of freedom he had as an American for granted, he confessed, ''I suppose it is, but I have to admit I've never thought of it like that. I just wanted to spend time with him and sight-seeing in Old City seemed like a good excuse.''

Holly smiled and shook her head. ''It might have been prudent to just say yes.''

Jim glanced down suddenly aware that Ian had come back to stand between them. The boy looked on, his big hazel eyes wide and curious. ''I don't lie, Holly,'' Jim said, seeking her gaze with his. ''Even about simple things. I hope you'll come to believe that about me in time.'' Jim looked away from his heart's desire and down at his son. ''So, Ian, want to go see some of Philadelphia's historical sights? As your mum just pointed out, as an American citizen, it's your heritage.''

''Oh!'' Ian gasped. ''That would be grand. Can I have a soft pretzel with that yellow mustard on it? And a steak sandwich for lunch? And water ice?''

Jim laughed. ''I said see Philly, not eat your way through it. Are you sure you can eat all of that?''

Ian threw his shoulders back proudly. ''Oh, absolutely. Mickey Osborne says the foods of Philadelphia are the best in the world. I want to try them all.'' He grimaced comically. ''Except perhaps scrapple. I asked what was in it and Mr. Osborne said everything the pig has to offer but the squeal! Gross!''

"Hey! Watch it," Jim protested ruffling Ian's thick crop of hair. "That's my favorite food. Not once in my thirty-four years have I found a more perfect food than scrapple."

Ian frowned, then straightened his shoulders like someone facing a firing squad. "Then I guess I must try it, as well."

Jim put his hand on his son's shoulder. "Relax, kid. It's a breakfast food. You're off the hook for a while. Let's take my truck since I know where we're headed and parking spots in Old City are at a premium." He turned to find Holly staring at him as if he'd grown another head. "Or not," he added, afraid he'd once again moved more swiftly than the Lord wanted. Let God, idiot, he growled to himself.

Holly shook her head and her eyes cleared a bit. "No. That's fine. City parking isn't my strong suit anyway. Your truck is fine."

Holly had thought Ian would sit between them, acting as a buffer, but Jim's truck had a little seat behind hers where Ian wanted to sit for its better view. She pressed up against the door as far from Jim as she could get. He glanced at her and frowned as he started the truck. "You'll have to move in farther on the seat and get your seat belt on, Holly. It's a state law. You buckle up back there too, sport," Jim said glancing in his rearview mirror.

Holly scooted over and buckled up trying to ignore what his nearness did to her as her fingers fumbled with the seat belt. "What shall we see first?" she asked as Jim put the car in gear. Holly was thankful for the distraction of the moving vehicle.

"That'll depend on where I find a parking spot. It would probably be best to find something near the Mall."

"We're going shopping?"

"*Independence* Mall," Jim said and chuckled at her in that oh-so-male way of his. He pulled up next to the cashier at the exit of the parking garage to pay the fee. "It's where Independence Hall and the Liberty Bell are," he continued as he pulled out into the heavy city traffic. "It's the heart of Old City. If I can grab a spot near there, we can hoof up to Ross House on Arch then double back and catch the Liberty Bell. On the way maybe we can get Ian that soft pretzel—"

"With mustard!" Ian added from behind.

"With mustard," Jim affirmed and glanced in the mirror again. She watched a look of such utter love soften his gaze as he beheld his son that tears sprang in her eyes. Had she been wrong to keep them apart all these years? If what she'd seen so far of the changes in Jim were true, she may have cheated her son of a wonderful father for years.

Aware suddenly of Jim's gaze on her, Holly blinked and looked at him. "What?" she asked.

Jim frowned. "I asked how that sounds to you?"

"Oh! Wonderful. It all sounds wonderful," she said hoping she hadn't agreed to anything she'd be sorry for later.

A horn beeped behind them and Jim looked away, starting the car forward. After inching along through the confusing weave of cars, buses, trucks and one-way streets, Jim smoothly put his vehicle into a spot Holly would never have attempted. "Okay, troops," Jim said as he hopped out of the pickup. "Let's load the meter up with quarters and be on our way."

What followed was an afternoon full of laughter and history. For someone who'd never thought of his heritage, Jim certainly knew his history. And what he didn't know the tour guides at the historic landmarks did. After they ate, Jim flagged down a horse-drawn carriage for a short riding tour. Tired and content, Ian slept all the way home.

Holly closed the door to Ian's room later that night, and, with a sigh, flopped down onto the wide comfy chair near the hearth. It had been a good day. Too good. And Jim had been a perfect companion. Too perfect. She picked up the throw pillow next to her and gave it a good solid punch. He seemed to be everything she'd always dreamed of in a man and in a husband.

How could that be? She knew firsthand the kind of man he was. She scowled at the floor. Or was that the kind of man he *had been?*

If there was one thing Holly hated in life, it was having second thoughts. And these last days had been full of second thoughts. Jim had been younger than she'd realized when they'd been married. Apparently he'd only been twenty-seven when she'd last seen him. She knew he'd been in the navy for nine years when they met but she'd assumed he was so much older than that. He'd certainly looked older, she thought defensively.

Now at thirty-five his dark hair had a few threads of silver and the creases around his eyes that had already been evident eight years ago were carved a little deeper. But he still looked like any woman's idea of a leading man—hers included!

Holly sank deeply into the cushy, overstuffed chair and hugged the recently abused pillow to her chest. She closed her eyes and her thoughts drifted. At first, they were filled with the unfairness of her still being attracted to the man who had so disordered her life. But soon she began to wonder what had made her think Jim was so much older than twenty-five when they'd met.

Her brow creased as she recalled him in those days. Handsome. Intelligent. Quiet. She'd been so proud that he'd chosen her. But then later, what she had thought was a quiet demeanor had turned out to be a haunted soul. What had stolen his youth? Drinking?

Or had there been a reason for the drinking and had that been the real problem? She was ashamed to admit even to herself that she'd never really cared about his life before they'd met. And she'd certainly never tried to get him to talk about what drove him to try drinking his problems away. She'd never even considered that there *was* an underlying problem. She'd just demanded he change.

She recalled Jim's smile when he'd dropped them off at her car and finally grasped what was so different about him now. His eyes were unshadowed. It was as if some deep hurt inside him had healed in the time since they'd parted. Had she been so self-centered back then that he'd needed to turn to a bottle instead of her to dull the pain she only now recognized?

Even young Ian had reached out and had at least learned where Jim had grown up. But as his wife, she hadn't even done that. That certainly didn't say much about her, did it?

I'm so sorry, Lord Jesus. I really did fail too, didn't I?

Maybe it was time she learned more about her son's father—for Ian's sake only, she assured herself. She wouldn't be doing it for herself to assuage her guilt or even to satisfy her curiosity. It was too late for any relationship between her and Jim other than as Ian's parents. But she should know what kind of life had produced her son's father.

Today watching Ian with Jim had been like watching a flower open. Ian craved his father's love and the affection Jim seemed able to give so easily. And Jim clearly needed his son's respect and love in return. She prayed for Ian's sake that the changes in Jim were real and permanent.

It was also obvious that the shrines of democracy they'd visited that day were as new to Jim as they had been to her and Ian even though as an American born and bred, he knew the general history. And while she found the places they visited interesting and Ian was awed by the symbols of liberty, Jim clearly found them inspiring.

His questions to their tour guides had been profound and incisive. He'd studiously written notes in the margins of the brochures they'd been given the same way people at her church did in their Bibles. When she'd asked why he was so interested, Jim had readily admitted that he'd been having a hard time with his Sunday sermon for the next week. It would be the Fourth of July.

Unlike her father, Jim apparently didn't follow a liturgical calendar with specific scriptures he'd be expected to expound upon each week. Instead he picked a book of the Bible and taught through it verse by verse, teaching life lessons as he found them within the sacred word. Only on special occasions did he pick a specific subject and preach topically the way her minister in New York did. It appeared that on Independence Day, their visit to Old City Philadelphia and the lessons it highlighted for Jim would be the subject of his sermon. She had to admit to wanting to hear what he had to say.

But did she want to attend services at his church? She'd seen the Web site and it looked like a fellowship she'd really enjoy. But she also knew that the feelings Jim always brought to the surface in her would interfere with her ability to worship properly. And she acknowledged further that it could be quite embarrassing if the people at the church connected her to Jim. In fact, now that she thought about it, they were sure to do just that.

The trouble was, of course, that Ian was expecting to attend Jim's church. Since finding Jim and later the Web site, Ian often spoke about the Tabernacle and all the wonderful programs Jim had arranged for its children. Maybe on Sunday she could send Ian to church with Maggie and Trent. That would give her a little longer to decide how Ian would react if she took him elsewhere.

No longer feeling as content as she had, Holly stood and went to the little galley kitchen to fix a nice cuppa hoping the warm tea would soothe her restless heart.

Chapter Six

It was probably two or three in the morning when Holly finally drifted off to sleep on the settee and not quite eight when a knock on the door woke her. She staggered over and opened it. Standing on the landing in the blinding sunlight were four children. All had hair in varying shades of red and freckles patterned across the bridges of their noses.

"Hi. I'm Mickey Osborne. Can Ian come out and play?" the tallest child asked.

"I'm afraid he's rather a slugabed in the mornings."

The oldest girl, the next step down in the quartet, gave a disappointed little groan, but, before Holly could assure her that Ian would be up and about soon, the younger boy frowned and spoke up.

"What's that mean? Slugabed? Does he squiggle all around in the bed and leave it all slimy?"

"Daniel," the girl groaned. "Don't start the torture so early in the day!"

Daniel put his hands on his narrow hips. "I only asked what she meant, Rachel. How can I understand her if I don't ask?"

Holly could have sworn slugabed was an expression she'd heard in America. She smiled. It could have been London. What had Winston Churchill said? Two nations separated by a common language. "I don't mind questions. Let's see, Daniel. A slug moves slowly and just sort of lies there doing almost nothing. So I suppose it means that Ian stays late in bed most mornings just lying around."

Daniel sighed. "Oh. You should'a just said that. Catch ya later, Mrs. D." He took the youngest girl's hand. "Come on, Gracie, let's go see if we can get Dad to help us fly our kite."

"You shouldn't have done that you know," Rachel said to Holly. "It only encourages him if you answer his dumb questions. Mom says the best thing to do is watch what you say around him and don't give him an opening. If you don't give him an opening, he won't get a shot at you. Well, we'll be around. When Ian gets up tell him he can find us and play with us. See you later, Mrs. Dillon."

The children turned and raced down the wooden steps and across the yard. Holly stared after them, confusion knitting her brow. Perhaps she just wasn't quite awake.

"Was that my new mates, Mum?" Ian asked, his voice sleepy and a little hoarse.

"Yes. A dizzying lot, aren't they?"

"I hadn't noticed. Perhaps because I mostly showed Daniel some things about his little computer. After that they took me upstairs to show me the incredible playrooms Mr. Osborne and Dad built for them on the third floor of their house. Then it was time for them to do their chores and Dad asked me to come here to help you unpack."

Holly nodded and walked into the little kitchen. "What would you like to eat?"

A few hours later Holly made her way across the yard and found all five children sitting on the back porch finishing off ice-cream bars. "Have you eaten already?" she asked, amazed that they were done when they'd only asked Ian to eat with them a quarter hour earlier.

"Their mum isn't well." Ian explained. "Mr. Osborne is making her take a nap and then he's going to make our lunch. He gave us our sweets first to hold us over."

"Okay, kids, come and get it," Trent called out and his little tribe responded instantly. Ian brought up the rear.

"Ian, I hope you like peanut butter and jelly," Trent was saying as she followed the children. "It's about all I'm good at in a pinch."

"Need any help?" Holly asked. "It looks as if you have your hands full here."

"You could try talking some sense into my wife," Trent growled, "I've got everything else handled."

"Talk sense to her? Trent, I've yet to meet her."

He gestured to the doorway. "Be my guest. Steps are through there. Last door at the end of the hall. Maybe she needs to hear from another woman that she should see a doctor."

"But I'm a stranger."

"Well, she isn't listening to me. Maybe hearing it from a stranger will knock a little sense into her. She's been sick on and off for weeks. And she's exhausted all the time."

"Is she going to go to heaven to be with my first mommy and daddy?" little Grace asked, her blue eyes wide and worried.

"I changed my mind. I want strawberry jelly," Daniel demanded as he stood.

Trent had instantly paled when Grace asked her question. He put a hand on Daniel's shoulder. "Kids, nothing's wrong with Maggie. She's a little under the weather. She'll be fine. Okay?"

Daniel nodded and sat back down. "I guess grape's fine. Sorry, Daddy. I don't want nothing to happen to Mom."

"Anything. You don't want *anything* to happen to her."

Daniel squinted up at his father. "Isn't that what I said?"

Holly hid a snicker. It was possible that she hadn't been that sleepy this morning after all. Daniel appeared to be quite a character!

"I'll go up and talk to her," Holly told Trent and retreated through the kitchen door. She made her way through a house so large it could have been a small hotel by New Zealand standards. After the cozy country kitchen the more formal areas were a surprise. They'd been lovingly restored with the kind of wallpaper and detail used in Victorian times.

She found the central staircase and followed the hall to the door Trent had said would lead her to Maggie. Standing outside the master suite, she stared at the heavy door and nearly turned away. Who was she to tell a stranger what to do? Then she remembered the fear in the eyes of those adorable children and in Trent's eyes, as well. Fear that he'd quickly masked for the sake of his children. She tapped shyly.

"Yes?" a muffled voice called.

Holly pushed the door open. "Hallo," she said as she saw the wan-looking woman in the bed sit up. She had a lovely face and even prettier chestnut hair. Only her skin tone told of some sort of illness. "I hope I'm not disturbing you. Trent sent me up. I'm Holly Dillon."

"Oh, Holly. No, of course, you aren't disturbing me. I'm so glad to meet you. The nap was Trent's idea. Jim's talked of nothing but you since he got back from New York...you and Ian, that is. Sit. Please. I don't think I'm contagious. No one else has gotten this." She waved her hand indicating the bed and herself. "Whatever this is that I've got."

"I'd love to sit and chat for a bit but I warn you I've been sent on a mission." Holly sat in the boudoir chair near the bed.

"Mission?"

"I'm to convince you to see a doctor."

Maggie Osborne sighed. "Trent. The man is a worrywart of the first water."

"To be fair, I think he may have a point. Your children are asking him questions like 'Is Mommy going to heaven?'"

Maggie's hand flew to her mouth as a look of horror widened her eyes. "Oh, dear. I hadn't thought. But this is so ridiculous. I'm sure it's nothing serious."

Holly stared at Maggie Osborne. Talk about not seeing the forest for the trees. "Have you considered the simplest answer? Perhaps you're expecting."

"Expecting?"

"A baby. Perhaps you're pregnant. It happens to women all the time."

A sad smile bloomed on Maggie Osborne's face. "Oh, I wish…but I'm afraid that isn't possible. I can't have children. Trent and I tried for years."

"Then I think you'd best seek a physician because something is wrong. Jim told me about your children and their parents. They're frightened of losing you."

"Oh, all right, I'll see a doctor. Hand me the phone. I'll call now and you can tell Trent your mission was a success. This is ridiculous."

After Maggie made her appointment, she handed Holly the phone and settled back against her mountain of pillows. "So tell me about yourself and how you met our pastor."

Holly stiffened. "I'd rather not. That's a period of my life I've put behind me."

"Isn't that sort of impossible? After all, there's Ian as a constant reminder."

"He's the only good thing that came out of that time. I was a foolish young girl blinded by a uniform and a handsome face. It's that simple. Jim Dillon wasn't always the paragon he appears to be now, I assure you."

Maggie's smile was mischievous. "Oh, I hope not. That would destroy the fantasies of so many women. One woman swears he was a spy. He's always looked a bit like he had a dangerous past."

"More like disreputable, actually."

"I know about his drinking problem."

"It would be easier to hear about than live with, I promise you."

"I don't doubt it. Look, Holly. Jim may be our friend but that doesn't mean I think he was perfect or is even now. He'd be the first to call me on it if I even implied that. We're all sinners."

Holly could see the sincerity in Maggie's brown eyes. "I'm just so afraid to do the wrong thing. You're a parent. You must see that I have reason to be leery of Jim being in Ian's life."

"Of course you have reason. He's talked about his drinking and the destruction it brought to his life often in sermons and in private with Trent and me. But I've known him for years. The changes you must see, compared to the man he says he once was, are very real. He's a good man. One you can count on to be a good father to his son."

"I sincerely hope so. Ian would be devastated if he

lost Jim now, but I will not allow my child to be endangered."

"I'm sure that won't happen. I want you to know that I'm here if you need a friend or a sounding board."

The realization hit Holly that, since leaving her girlhood friend behind in Australia when she agreed to travel with the ambassador, she hadn't had a real friend. And she suddenly felt the lack deeply. Now more than ever, Holly needed someone to talk to. "Thank you, Maggie. I could use a friend."

It was nearly midnight on Wednesday night by the time Jim finished vacuuming and cleaning up after the church's midweek Bible study. The child care rooms were always the worst of the mess but he didn't care. He grinned and shook his head, putting the last barrel of plastic blocks up on the shelf in the second-grade room. As far as he was concerned, offering special programs for children was the most important function a church could provide.

Minutes later, the sanctuary and all the classrooms having been locked up for the night, Jim opened the door to his little two-room portion of the old barn that housed the church. Without even undressing, he sank onto the bed and was so tired he felt as if he might sink right on through it. He wondered absently how different his life would have been if from childhood he'd known the name of Jesus as something other than a curse. There had been so much pain and hopelessness in his life that he would never have felt. He would have known his Father in heaven loved him all those nights when he'd lain in his bed wondering why his earthly father hadn't loved him enough to stay. Hunger might not have seemed so eternal, either, if he'd understood eternity.

He might never have taken that first drink.

Jim shook his head and lay back, lacing his fingers behind his head. It was a mistake to try rethinking the past. It was a futile exercise. Had he known Jesus, he might never have gone in the navy, might never have met Holly and wouldn't have Ian in his life now. He'd never have started a Bible study among his fellow AA members and the Tabernacle would never have been born. And then there were all the souls he'd reached through the AA program the Tabernacle sponsored now. Add to them all those who'd come forward over the years every time he'd given an altar call and those saved because of the witness of changed lives of church members.

No, the Lord had a plan for everyone's life. And Jim knew he was living the life he was meant to live. He just had to trust that the big picture of his life held something good to counteract the pain he felt every time he said goodbye to Ian and every time he looked into Holly's eyes and saw wariness instead of love.

He hadn't seen Ian or Holly since Monday and missed both of them terribly. He didn't know how that was possible considering that before last week he hadn't seen either of them for years. But miss them he did.

Jim sat up, knowing he had to undress for bed but

the phone rang before he got even one button of his shirt undone. *Lord, don't let this be bad news.* But it was. Jake Testa, Jim's friend and the man who'd been instrumental in the start of the Tabernacle had suffered a heart attack.

The sun was coming up when he made his way through the rabbit warren of corridors at Paoli Memorial on his way back home. He took an often used shortcut that would skirt the ER, grateful for any shortening of the distance to his truck. He was nearly sleep-walking by the time he pushed open the door near the ER waiting room.

"You're a little late."

The irate voice chased the drowsiness in a split second as alarm and then adrenaline flooded his system. Jim blinked. "Holly? What is it? Is there something wrong with Ian?"

"I left a message on your answering machine when you didn't answer your phone. Ian's had another attack. He's fine now, no thanks to support from his father. I just finished with the paperwork. They're about to release him. He asked for you all night, Jim. I'd have thought you'd be home at two in the morning. Or at least three or four. I gave up trying to reach you about then."

It was clear that she thought he'd been out drinking up a storm in some bar. Jim beat back his temper but just barely. He knew how he looked, his beard heavy, his eyes red from tears he'd been forced to hold back, his hair rumpled. He told himself that to Holly this must have seemed like a replay of too many other nights when she'd had to track him down, especially the night their marriage went up in flames.

He took one more calming breath. "Normally, I would have been home, Holly, but I've been here with a member of the church since after midnight."

Holly had the good grace to blush. "Oh. I'm sorry. Is everything all right?"

A bittersweet agony engulfed him. Once again he blinked back threatening tears. "That depends on your perspective, I guess. For Jake, it is. The pain's gone now and he's passed on into glory. As for the rest of us, his family and friends, we'll grieve his loss then go on with the help of the Lord and the knowledge that we'll see him again one day."

"I'm sorry I misunderstood and I'm sorry for your loss. Is he—was he—someone you were close to?"

"He was one of the original members of the church. There wouldn't be a Tabernacle if he hadn't helped me with getting the church started in those early days. Actually, it was more like Jake started it by wrangling me into starting the Bible study that grew into the church. He was one of a kind."

"Here's Ian," a young woman said from the doorway to the ER treatment rooms. "I see you finally reached his father." Jim turned to see the familiar face of Trudy, one of the ER nurses he saw all too often. "Oh, Pastor Jim. I didn't recognize you at first. How's Mr. Testa?"

"Dad! You came!" Ian shouted and ran up to him, hugging him around the waist.

Jim looked down into the adoring eyes of his son. At least Ian hadn't assume the worst. "Actually I didn't know you were here till just now, sport. I was here before you so I never got your mum's messages. One of the members of my church was very sick last night and I spent it at his bedside." He looked up from Ian's blatant adoration to answer the young nurse's question. "Jake's gone to be with the Lord. This latest attack was just too much for his heart."

"I was afraid of that. He seemed like such a nice man. I'm glad you could be with him." She bit her lip and looked at the floor then back up. "Listen, I've been thinking about what you said about death not being so big a deal if you know where you're headed next. I see a lot of death here and it gets you thinking. You know? Where is this Tabernacle again?"

Oh, Jake, you would have loved this, Jim thought, fighting a wistful grin as he fished a business card out of his wallet. "Service times and directions are on there. Hope to see you."

She looked at it then and smiled. "Thanks. I really think I'll come." She started to back away. "Well, thanks again, I'd better get back. My shift's almost over. Bye, Ian, I hope you know what a lucky kid you are to have such a great dad."

"Oh, do I ever," Ian said and squeezed Jim around the waist again.

Jim felt his eyes mist again but for a joyful reason this time. He cleared his throat. "How'd you find the hospital?" he asked Holly. "I meant to show you how to get here."

"As a precaution, Maggie told me how to come here yesterday."

"So you have your car with you. I'll walk you out. Need a lift to the car, sport?" he asked Ian.

Ian shook his head. "You look all done in, Dad," he said gravely. "I think I best walk."

Jim ran a hand over his face feeling the scrape of the dark beard. He probably looked like five miles of bad road. Grinning down at his wise son, he quipped, "I think you just may be right. It's long past time for me to hit the sack."

At the car, after Ian scrambled into the back seat, Holly turned to face Jim. "I'm really sorry for misjudging you."

"I can't pretend it didn't hurt or make me angry but I shouldn't have been surprised. You don't trust me yet. But it did point out the problem of your not being able to get in touch with me. I think it's time I start carrying a beeper or maybe even a cell phone. I'll see to it later today and call with the number. Will I see you and Ian at church Sunday?"

"Uh…" She hesitated, her green eyes uncertain. "Won't it be a little awkward for you having your ex-wife there?"

"Not in the least. I hadn't even considered being embarrassed by you or Ian. Everyone knows about both of you. They've known for years that my dependence on alcohol really messed up my life and recently I told them all about our marriage and the son I'd finally found. What's left to be embarrassed about?" *Except a huge case of unrequited love for a woman I hurt so badly that she can't trust me, let alone love me.*

"I'll think seriously about bringing him."

"Okay, then. If you come to the last service, I'll have time afterward to show you two around." Jim bent down and looked into the car. "See you, Son." Later he didn't know why he did what he did but as he stood up, he casually kissed Holly goodbye, turned and left without another word. He somehow managed not to whistle his way to his truck.

Chapter Seven

Jim spent the next half hour kicking himself for that wonderful impulsive kiss that had felt anything but casual once his lips touched hers. But as wonderful as it had felt, it had been just plain stupid. And he knew he should never have done it. What, he chided himself time and time again, had happened to letting God work on Holly's heart? What had happened to not rushing her?

Why had he done it?

Then when he climbed into bed at last, he spent the next half hour before exhaustion claimed him trying to relive that precious moment. Her lips were as silky today as they'd been all those years ago, and her scent was still as light as springtime.

The trouble with spending time with his ex-wife, he decided, was that he knew *exactly* where his desire could lead and how it would feel to get there. He knew *exactly* what it was he was missing. And when he fell asleep and dreamed, it wasn't what could be that filled his mind but what had been.

And when he woke alone knowing she was lost to him, his heart broke all over again.

The following two days Jim drove himself harder than usual, trying to outrun those tormenting dreams at night and the even more agonizing daydreams. On Saturday he performed Jake Testa's memorial service in the early morning.

He spent every other waking hour, working in the summer heat, on an old building that sat at the back of the property. Like the barn, it was constructed using the same historic timber frame method he'd found in the barn that had become the Tabernacle.

Jim was once again drawn to give a second chance to something that time and the elements had nearly destroyed. It was what the Lord had done for him, after all. To Jim, the building quickly became a symbol of the marriage he prayed God would renew. He knew also that he didn't deserve that chance. But neither had he deserved salvation, and the Lord had granted that even greater gift. So he worked nearly around the clock, trying to stay away from Holly so God could work on her heart without His bumbling servant's attempts to hurry things along.

"Mind telling a friend what you think you're doing?" Jim heard Trent Osborne shout up to him. Jim looked down the twenty or so odd feet to the ground where his friend stood in the shadow of what was left of the roof. Jim grabbed the beam above his head when the ground swam before his eyes.

Knowing he needed a break, he climbed across the rafters to the ladder that led to the ground. "Numbering the pieces. I finally decided what to do with it and the county called again to complain that it's a hazard with all the kids coming out here," Jim said hopping down to the dirt floor. "So, I decided to move the frame to a few hundred feet from the main building. With the population explosion at the church, the nursery overflowed into the teens' space a couple months ago."

"Is that why you had that new pad poured?"

Jim nodded. "I had the concrete delivered late yesterday."

"Who helped you form it and put in the rebar?"

"I did the forms and rebar late on Wednesday and early Thursday morning. In the afternoon, the concrete truck came to pour it and the driver helped me float it. Gifford's donated the concrete, so it won't cost the treasury—"

"Whoa!" Trent put up his hand traffic-cop style. "Jim, I'm not questioning what another building will do to the church's funds. I'm questioning what it'll do to *you*. It's been ninety-five and above every day this week and I won't even mention this steam-bath humidity. So, what are you up to?"

"Yesterday after Jake Testa's service and today I've been numbering the posts and beams and trus—"

Jim broke off when Trent folded his arms and

scowled. The man could really get to you with that look. He had four kids and a wife to practice on.

Jim sighed. "I guess you could say I'm staying away from Holly, trying to let God work in her heart. In the meantime, I guess I took a page out of your book. Your old one. I'm keeping too busy to think. Awake or asleep."

"Am I right in assuming this doesn't have a lot to with losing Jake?"

Jim pursed his lips and shook his head. Losing Jake had been a blow but the constant reminder of all he'd lost with Holly felt like an anchor tugging him under.

"Having Holly near is really doing a number on you, isn't it?" Trent said as he sat on a makeshift bench Jim had rigged out of a fallen beam.

Jim pulled his ball cap off and sank down onto the same long beam next to Trent. As he leaned his forearms on his thighs, he stared at the ground, feeling weighted down and suddenly exhausted.

"I love her. I can hardly remember not loving her. When we met, I thought I wasn't good enough for her so I invented this persona of her ideal man. Being American and in uniform helped a lot. I was a savior. Her ticket out of a pretty messed-up home life. That man was the man she loved and he was the man she married."

He scrubbed his jaw with his hand and went on. It was still hard to believe how messed up his thinking had been in those days. "A couple weeks after the wedding, I realized I couldn't keep up the act forever. So rather than letting her see the real me, I started drinking heavily and pushed her away. And then I drank more to hide from the pain of watching her realize I wasn't who she thought I was. And so she got sadder and madder, and she loved me less every day. It was like watching the most brilliant star in the sky dim night after night knowing that once it went out completely it would be dead. The twisted thing about it is that even when I was nearly destroying her, it was because I loved her so much."

Trent sighed and gazed at the horizon before turning back to Jim. "You know in another sense I did the same thing to Maggie. Withholding information. Keeping secrets. Did you ever tell Holly the stories about your childhood that you've told here in sermons?"

"No, but I doubt she cares now. When I should have told her, I was afraid she'd see what a flawed person I was. I really don't think she ever loved *me*. But it wasn't her fault. I rushed her into marriage because I was afraid I'd lose her. I never gave her a chance to know me." Jim pressed his lips together for a moment then continued. "Fear is a terrible thing, Trent. It weighs us down until we either cry out for help or we break. I was too much of a coward or too stupid to reach out, so I broke."

Trent gripped his shoulder and squeezed. "If God could put Maggie and me back together, He can do the same thing for you and Holly."

Jim felt his friend's support and was heartened by it. But he didn't think Trent understood what he was trying to say. "I've thought about this a lot these last few days. I guess this isn't the kind of activity that keeps your mind from working after all.''

Trent looked around at all the work Jim had done and chuckled. ''You should have asked me before you risked heatstroke. Don't you remember that it was while I worked on Paradise Found that I thought out all the mistakes I'd made with Maggie?''

Jim smiled a little at his own foolishness. ''Well, it worked the same way for me. And what I realized is that God may not have much to work with. Holly not only doesn't love me or trust me, she still doesn't even *know* me. You and Maggie still loved each other and you only had one secret.''

''It was a huge secret, Jim, and I kept it for ten years. Aren't you the one always saying, 'There's nothing too big for the Lord'? I don't see the harm in letting Holly get to know the real you. Maybe God doesn't want Holly to fall back in love with the man she once *thought* you were. Maybe He wants her to fall in love for the first time with the man you *are*. For that to happen you can hardly go on hiding from her.''

Jim shook his head and grinned sheepishly. ''It's a little humbling to have you repeating my own words to me and making so much sense with them. Thanks, Trent. I think you may have a point.''

Trent laughed and gave Jim a shove as they both stood. ''Of course I do.''

Jim set his ball cap on the back of his head. ''So what brought you out here? You never did say.''

Trent's lips tipped up into an odd, almost perplexed

smile. "We're having a little impromptu celebration out at Paradise Found. I called the church office and Mrs. White told me you'd all but buried yourself out here. So I came over to ask you in person and find out what you were up to."

"Celebration? Oh! For the Fourth."

"Not really. Remember that population explosion in the church you mentioned?"

"Yeah," Jim answered and frowned. Now where was this going?

Trent put his hands in his back pockets and rocked back on his heels. He grinned again. "Maggie's not sick, Jim. She's pregnant."

Jim blinked. "What? I thought the doctors said you two couldn't have kids."

Trent's grin widened. "What was it we were saying about no problem being too big for the Lord?"

Holly turned when she heard a car door slam. She knew Trent had returned with Jim before she even turned around. She'd always had some weird sort of radar where her ex-husband was concerned. And it annoyed her! It said something about her and her feelings for him that she just didn't want to deal with. But, as she watched him pick up her son and swing him high in the air as he walked across the lawn, Holly acknowledged that she had little choice but to deal with those feelings.

They were feelings that had resurfaced with her first glimpse of him in her New York flat. And they'd progressed since. What was the matter with her? That kiss for instance. She should have been angry. Fortunately or unfortunately, Holly was honest enough to admit to herself that she hadn't been angered by the quick kiss but by his absence since. And she was also honest enough to admit that she was confused about why that was.

So here she was watching him walk toward Maggie, not knowing her own mind and trying to figure out what was in his. Was he trying to keep her off balance? Or was he as knocked off-kilter as she was?

She watched him hug Maggie and imagined he was offering congratulations and probably prayers. Prayer seemed to be a big part of Jim's life these days.

Then, as he turned away from Maggie, a score of children took off across the yard toward him calling, "Pastor Dillon," as they closed the distance. It was a clear case of hero-worship with all of them. They quite simply swarmed all over him and he wound up wrestling on the ground with them.

The scene troubled Holly as no revelation about Jim had to that point. His love of all children, not just his own son, rode the current of the summer breeze in the joy of his laughter and shone in the two-hundred-watt smile she could see even at a distance.

You robbed both of them of this. He said he's been sober for six years. They could have had each other all this time.

Holly turned away when a second even more painfully treacherous thought invaded what was left of her peace. *You could have had him in your life, too. You failed Ian. You failed yourself and Jim. But worse, you failed God. You never even tried to help your own husband. You kept silent about the One who could have helped him fight his alcoholism. Instead you turned your back on God and your husband.*

Holly buried the accusation as deeply in her heart as she could. She'd been protecting Ian! Rather than risk more errant thoughts, she turned back to watch her son. Ian got to his feet, laughing and put his hand out as if to pull Jim to his feet. Jim took the offered hand and got to his feet. Then Ian led his father over to where Grace and Daniel Osborne were.

She couldn't help but watch the way Jim walked and stood as several more children joined the small band. The little girl seemed upset and Daniel put a comforting arm around his little sister. Before Holly blinked an eye they all trooped into the woods leaving Daniel comforting Grace. Jim looked for all the world like a version of the Pied Piper when he returned some minutes later, something small, black and furry held gently in his strong arms.

Curious and drawn to him, she went to investigate, pushing away the guilt she felt for her attraction to him. "What have they involved you in?" she asked Jim, glad of the impersonal subject considering her growing attraction and the unsettling way they'd parted.

"It's a kitten, Mum," Ian told her. "The kids got it the day after we arrived."

"She wandered away and they wanted me to help find her." He stooped down and put the tiny creature in Grace Osborne's arms. "Now you take Skunk and put her inside in her box. And don't take her out again unless your mommy or daddy say you can. Okay?''

Grace nodded. ''Okay, Pastor Jim. Thank you for finding her. I love her so much and I waited so long to get her.''

''What kind of name is Skunk for a kitten?'' Holly just had to ask. These Osborne children really were a curious lot.

Jim chuckled as the troop moved toward the house. ''When she was two, Grace mistook a baby skunk for a kitten. Trent barely got it away from her without the two of them getting sprayed. I understand he promised her a kitten that day and she's never let him forget it. Maggie finally caved in.''

''I've noticed raising four children is a bit complicated. Of late I've begun feeling as if I'm an imposter to parenthood. I get flustered with only one child to look after. I don't know how Maggie will cope with another.''

''With great aplomb, I assure you. A house full of children was always Maggie's dream.'' Jim glanced away to where Ian stood. ''So how *has* Ian been? Sounds as if he's been a handful.''

''No. Not really. He's having the time of his life here. I thought perhaps you would have called. A-about Ian,'' she added hastily wishing she could take her comment back.

Jim grimaced. ''He was at church with Maggie and Trent Wednesday night so I saw him then. But to tell you the truth, I've been trying to stay away. From you. Not from Ian. I'm sorry about the kiss, Holly. It felt right at the time but then it seemed as if I'd over-stepped. I buried myself in work these past few days trying to give you time.''

Holly ignored his apology, not willing to explain that there was nothing to be sorry for. Instead, determined to find out more about this man who had fathered her son, she replied with a question. ''What kind of church work have you been doing?''

''You really want to know?'' Jim asked and at her nod he gestured toward a couple of Adirondack chairs under a nearby tree. Holly looked around guiltily but again pushed away the irrational feeling. She was only exploring her feelings and trying to learn more about this man. She was trying to protect her son, not endanger him.

As she moved toward the little enclave under the sweeping limbs of the willow, Jim smiled. Holly saw something unreadable in his expression that was more than simple relief for the moment of rare accord. Holly's pulse jumped, when as they sat, his knee brushed hers. In the space of a glittering second, she realized too late that this time of harmony could very easily endanger her heart.

Chapter Eight

"I was working on a church building," Jim said dragging Holly out of her musings.

Holly blinked. "Building?" What were they talking about? Oh! His work! "I thought you'd already built the church building. It's a converted barn. Right?"

"That's been finished for a few years, for the most part. But there's another smaller timber frame building at the back of the property."

"Timber frame? That's special?"

"Timber framing is a kind of building style. It's considered historic. But the county still wants this one demolished. It isn't safe as it stands but not because the skeleton isn't as sturdy as the day it was built. The sheathing on the walls is rotted and the roof is falling in. So when the county called again Thursday morning, I decided if I wanted to save it I'd better get at it."

The boyish enthusiasm in Jim's eyes was something she would never have attributed to the controlled sailor she'd married. "By yourself?" she asked, noticing that he looked a bit tired even in his excitement.

He shrugged. "I've been numbering the pieces for the past day and a half so I can take it apart and put it back together after it's moved. When Trent came to invite me today, he promised to organize church members for a mini barn raising next month."

Holly studied him for a moment. "And what would you have done had he not stopped by today? Done it all by yourself?"

A sheepish expression took over Jim's face. "Maybe."

Holly had to bite back the urge to lecture him on taking care of himself. "What will you do with the building?" she asked instead. It was none of her concern if he overdid. He was a big boy who'd always been self-sufficient as far as she knew.

"The Tabernacle nursery had to be split and the older babies are now in the teen space most of the time. There's an advantage to it because the teens have chipped in to help and they've learned firsthand what a huge responsibility children are. But they also need a private space and the time to talk about the pressure they come under every day. It's tough for them to live in a world hostile to ideas like sobriety and celibacy and honoring God in their daily lives."

"It must be difficult. I'm not looking forward to Ian facing those choices and pressures. As difficult as being a parent is now, the teenage years scare me silly.''

Jim groaned comically. "Don't remind me. I haven't even gotten used to him being a growing boy. I guess he stayed a baby in my mind all these years.''

Though he'd started out joking, Holly saw a degree of pain creep into his eyes and her earlier guilt came rushing back. Had there been another way to keep Ian safe? Had she gone too far when she'd cut Jim wholesale from his son's life? "I imagine you think I should have let you know where we were going.''

Jim shook his head. "Holly, you were acting in Ian's best interest. I'm an alcoholic who was drinking heavily when you saw me last. For well over a year you were right to keep me from him. You had no way of knowing that I'd found the Lord and gotten my life together or for that matter that I cared where the two of you were. Don't start second-guessing yourself now. What I lost, I lost because of my sin. It was your job to protect Ian the way neither of us were protected as children. And you've done a wonderful job of it.''

Holly nodded. He was right. Ian was a wonderful child. "Sometimes I think he's more a miniature adult than a child,'' she admitted and laughed. "This morning I got a fifteen-minute lecture on sun safety and the proper use of sunblocks in the American sun.'' Holly noticed for the first time that Jim himself was sporting a rather bad sunburn. "And speaking of sun safety…'' she said looking pointedly at his arms.

Jim put his hand up in surrender. "Hey! I got the

heatstroke lecture from Trent already. As for the burn, it looks worse than it is.'' He slapped his reddened arm. ''See? It doesn't even hurt. I was working up in the rafters and the roof had already blown off in the section I was numbering. I didn't realize how long I'd been up there exposed until Trent showed up. What I have left to mark is undercover. Then I'll start pulling off what's left of the roof and walls. That ought to get the county off my back.''

''That's good,'' Holly said absently, her mind having slipped back a few pieces of dialogue. ''Jim, what did you mean about your parents not protecting you?''

Jim sat back and closed his eyes for several lengthy seconds. When he looked at her again, he looked uncertain. ''My father disappeared when I was too young to think more than that I'd done something to make him leave. My mother drank. She always got up and went to work, but she started drinking again before she came home. My sister Joan more or less raised me but she was only two years older than I was. My mother threw too much responsibility on her. You know about that firsthand having lived a similar life. But Joanie didn't react the way you did.''

He sighed, clearly still hurting from the memories. ''I don't know when Joanie started doing drugs but by the time she was thirteen I knew she was an addict. One day the police came to the door. She had overdosed. My mother was passed out drunk, so I went to the hospital with the police. Joanie died a few hours later. She was still only sixteen years old.

"They put me in a foster home. It was wonderful. Mrs. Dunbar had been married to a guy in the navy. He'd died in Vietnam. A hero. His pictures were everywhere. She had older kids and the way they talked about him made me want to be like him. It was terrific but it only lasted a few months. My mother managed to convince the authorities that I should be with her. They sent me back."

"I'm so sorry. I always thought—" Holly broke off. He had never talked about his life. And she had just presumed he'd stepped out of an all-American fairy tale, the kind she'd seen in old reruns on the telly. "Leave it to Beaver" and "Happy Days" come to life. "I assumed you came from a family so much more stable than mine."

"Please don't feel guilty. It isn't your fault what you assumed. It's what I let you assume. When I met you, I pretended to be from the kind of family I'd spent that time with. I pretended to be the kind of person you thought I was. When we arrived in Christchurch, we were warned by our commanding officer about local girls who thought Americans had hung the moon because we had money to spend on them. You wanted out and I could be your ticket. It was in your eyes that first night we met."

"I'm sorry. My girlfriends dragged me there that night with just that in mind. And I guess I did think of you as a knight in shining armor. But I did come to love you."

Jim flinched as if she'd struck him. "As I said, there's nothing to be sorry for. I didn't care why you were interested in me. You smiled and all I could think was how incredibly innocent and sweet you were and how wonderful it would be to have someone like you in my life. Everything I'd ever had was tarnished by where I grew up and the way I was raised. I wanted you no matter what. I knew you thought I'd come from some picture-perfect, American family."

"But I assumed wrong."

"The truth is that my mother finally managed to let drinking kill her when I was a senior in high school. I hid her death from school authorities, graduated and forged her signature to join the navy at seventeen right out of high school. I wasn't about to let her steal my dream."

"How did you hide her death?"

He squeezed his eyes tightly shut. When he opened them again she could still see in his hazel eyes the sheen of tears that he tried to hide by looking away. "She passed out in an alley and froze to death on her way home from a bar. I heard it on the news, and I knew it was her, but I never tried to claim her body. I let my own mother be buried as a Jane Doe four months and two days shy of my high school graduation. I had a job and managed to scrape together enough to keep from being evicted from our apartment till then."

"And you still feel guilty about that?"

"Wouldn't you?"

"No. You went when Joan was dying and you were only fourteen so it isn't as if you were a coldhearted boy. Jim, you owed your mother nothing. She gave you nothing.''

''She gave me life. All the authorities would have done was put me in a foster care again. I still would have gotten my diploma and been able to enlist in the navy. But I wanted to do it my way. I didn't want them putting me somewhere with new people I'd have to lose. I was wrong. She was my mother. She may not have fulfilled her obligations to me, but that didn't relieve me of my obligation to her. We're commanded to honor our parents.''

''Then you think I should love my father after the way he abandoned his children to a woman who eventually killed two of them?''

Jim shrugged. ''What I think isn't the question. It's what we're told to do. It's like forgiveness. We're not told to *feel* forgiveness. We're told to forgive. It's for us, not the other person. Your father was wrong. He cared more about his position than he cared for the welfare of his three children or his wife, for that matter. If it helps, he knows he was wrong.''

Holly stared at him. ''How do you know?''

''Because when I went back to New Zealand the first time, your father is where I started looking for you. It wasn't pleasant,'' he said sadly. ''He blamed me for taking you away. He blamed me for Alan's and Christie's deaths because they wouldn't have been with their mother if they'd been with you. It was the hardest day I've had since I got sober. I actually stood outside a pub. I was so tempted to forget the Lord and just bag it. But with His help, I finally walked on by.''

He'd almost drank. Holly found his admission disquieting but she pushed the worry to the back of her mind. "That wasn't fair of Father. Alan and Christie are dead because my mother killed them in a wreck. It was Mother and Father's fault. It doesn't sound as if he knows he was wrong or as if he's changed at all. Except that he blamed me the day of the funeral and now he's turned it onto you."

"Actually the Lord used me to spur the change in him. Before he'd launched into me, I'd told him about my conversion and that I'd been sober for over a year. Later that day one of his friends saw me standing outside that pub and he told your father. I guess the Lord spoke to George and made him see his unfairness. He was worried that I'd fallen off the wagon because of him and he went looking for me."

"Did he find you?"

Jim shook his head. "But when I went back two years later looking for you, I learned that he'd moved. He's running a mission much like the one in Riverside where I found the Lord. He's a changed man, Holly. He regrets his mistakes and wants desperately to have a relationship with you and Ian."

"I don't know." Holly bit her lip. Her father didn't hate her anymore. But how did she feel about him? "You have no idea what my life was like. Not only did I have to help hide Mother's drinking and take care of the little ones and keep the house perfect, but I had to score good grades in school as well. After all it wouldn't do if the daughter of the local minister wasn't top of the class. I lived in a world that felt like a pressure cooker."

"I know a little of what you went through because I watched Joanie cave in under less stress than you withstood. Holly, you can do anything you put your mind to. You're the strongest woman I've ever met. I know it doesn't mean a hill of beans to you but I'm proud of you and all you've accomplished for yourself and Ian."

Holly saw the sincerity in his eyes and was touched. "It does mean something, Jim. I'm not sure what or why, but it does. I'll think about my father. It would be hard to forgive him, even just deciding to and not feeling it, but I will try."

"Mum. Dad. Mr. Osborne says to come eat," Ian called as he ran toward them at a dead run.

"Oh! I should have offered to help Maggie."

"Relax. Maggie's mother is here. You wouldn't get within fifty feet of the kitchen with her around. She's an even better cook than Maggie." Jim stood and offered her a hand up out of the low chair.

Jim walked at Holly's side toward Trent and Maggie's back porch. He was still a little shocked at how well their conversation had gone. Holly hadn't run in shock from his revelations. She'd been kind and sympathetic. Why he'd thought she would act differently considering her own history, he didn't know. Maybe he still felt the stigma of his youth more than was rational. That was why he always stressed the importance of good parenting in family counseling sessions. Children took on the mantle of their environment and often carried the scars of childhood to their graves.

And like Joanie and almost himself, they were all too often early graves.

When they reached the back porch where Trent had set up several tables, Jim was disappointed to see that the men had gravitated to one table and the women and children to the others. Maggie and then her mother handed him plates laden with some of everything there was to eat, and he accepted the inevitable. He hadn't wanted their interlude to end but he'd done what Trent had suggested. Maybe it was enough for today.

Several hours later as the impromptu celebration began to break up, Jim settled on the ground and leaned against a tree trunk to rest his eyes for a few minutes. He had drifted off when Holly shook his shoulder.

"Jim. Wake up. Trent asked me to drive you home. Maggie's all done in and he wants to help with children's bedtime. Ian's staying here as well. Trent seemed to think you were too exhausted to wait for him to be free. I take it he was right."

"I'd really appreciate the lift as long as it isn't too much trouble," he admitted readily and couldn't stifle a wide yawn. "I may have overdone it a bit."

Holly chuckled. "No trouble. Besides I should see this church everyone is talking about. So, are you ready to set out?"

"Oh. More than ready. Let me just say goodbye to Trent and Maggie and I'll be right with you."

Minutes later as he approached the car, Jim blessed Trent and his support. The chance for a few more moments with Holly felt like a priceless treasure. But in the confines of the small car, silence reigned except for the occasional direction he needed to give Holly. It wasn't an uncomfortable silence. She just didn't seem inclined to talk and he was so tired that he couldn't get his brain to engage. Finally, as they drove onto church property, Holly asked him how he'd gotten the Tabernacle started.

"It's been the Lord's work from the beginning. I got a job with Jake Testa's construction company. He's the guy who died earlier in the week."

"You said he'd been a founding member and something about his talking you into the original Bible study."

Jim nodded, heartened that Holly had remembered. "I started telling the guys on the job sites about Jesus because I wanted them to experience His joy and love. Several of them asked to join the AA study I was already doing. I was uncomfortable with the idea, because they had different lives from the people in the study. But no one else was available to teach them so I said I'd give it a shot. Before I knew it there were too many people to fit in my apartment. Jake was one of the men who attended the study so he offered his home.

"After a few months Jake suggested we meet on Sunday mornings. But pretty soon his place started getting crowded, too, so we rented a fire hall. That wasn't a very permanent solution, though." He laughed. "Especially when the fire alarm went off and I had to either stop or shout over it. The people in the Bible study, most of whom I knew through construction, decided we should band together and buy a plot of land for a church. Jake found one on a farm near his place. The idea was to put up a church by ourselves as we could afford it.''

"That sounds like a long wait for your church, especially with you having to shout over the fire whistle.''

"Not from my perspective. I hadn't even acknowledged that we *were* a church. Or that I was the pastor.''

"Why? It sounds as if you were.''

Jim shrugged. "I guess I was afraid and feeling unworthy. I just couldn't grasp the idea that they wanted *me* to pastor their church. Or that the Lord would want me to pastor *His* church after all the wrong I'd done. But by then, the idea and the membership were like a snowball rolling down a snowy hill in one of those old cartoons. It was picking up speed and size and I was stuck right in the middle.

"Jake finally had to drag me out to look at the piece of land that we'd gotten for a song because I wouldn't go see it. I had my eyes closed so tight I was seeing stars, trying to put off the moment of truth.

"But he just kept on talking, giving me a running commentary on the scenery as we bumped along this drive we're on now. It used to be a narrow, rut-infested dirt road that led to the land we'd bought. It was sort of symbolic I guess, because I still had my eyes shut tight against this movement of the Lord.''

He laughed. At himself. At his sweaty palms as he revealed yet more of himself to the woman he loved. At the still seeming absurdity of God using a drunk to bring souls to Him.

"Well, I'd gotten about as carsick as I could get without completely embarrassing myself when I opened my eyes in self-defense."

As Holly pulled into the parking lot, Jim gestured to the horizon where the church now sat in all its rustic splendor. "And there it stood in the distance...this falling-down wreck of a barn right smack in the middle of our parcel."

Holly laughed as he'd hoped she would. "Then what?" she asked with surprising enthusiasm.

"I got out of the car and started walking toward it. I don't know what my face looked like, but Jake jumped out, too, and followed me. He kept telling me to calm down and that it was going to be fine. That we could tear it down with no problem. 'Tear it down?' I yelled. 'It's perfect!'"

Jim turned in the little car and faced Holly who had stopped at the back end of the parking lot. "Jake thought I was nuts but it *was* perfect. Well, okay, it was a mess at the time," he told her honestly. "But it had the most beautiful timber framing I'd ever seen. I knew I was meant to preserve it. I could see a church formed around that crude frame. Just the way the Lord had formed a church around this crude frame."

"And your church was born that day."

Jim chuckled. "Actually it had been born six months before that first Sunday we were at the fire house. Jesus had just waited to tell me till He knew I could handle it. Any sooner and I'd have run in the other direction just like Jonah did when God sent him to Nineveh. I thank Him every day for all He's done for me and for finding a better way than having a fish swallow me and spit me out three days later to get me to do His will.''

Holly laughed again. It was a musical sound that rang along his nerve endings. She cocked her head to the side, still smiling. ''Are you too worn-out to give me the nickel tour?''

Grateful for the distraction, Jim opened his door. ''I'm never too tired to show off this place. Especially to someone I care about. Come on.''

What followed was the most enjoyable half hour in his recent memory. Finally there was something he was proud of in his life that he could share with her. He told her about how he'd worked with the architect to bring the vision the Lord had given him alive. He showed her the little things he'd done that had transformed a barn into a place of love and peace that honored the Lord.

And throughout the tour one overwhelming truth sang in his soul. It felt right to walk into the sanctuary with her by his side.

He walked back in after escorting Holly to her car and stared up at the rough hewn cross that hung on the wall behind the podium. He remembered the day he'd fashioned it from a couple of stray beams and hung it there. No work had begun on the barn yet, and they'd renovated around the cross.

Even then the Lord had been in this place.

Please, Lord, he prayed. *Please give her back to me. I need her at my side.*

Chapter Nine

Ian settled into bed between Mickey and Daniel Osborne as Mr. Osborne checked under the bed and in the closet pretending to chase away the monsters that Gracie was sure were waiting to get her. She and Rachel were in the other guest room bed ready to conclude their pajama party.

"Okay. All checked out, sweetheart," Mr. Osborne said as he closed the closet door. "No monsters left. Boy howdy, did they ever run when they saw me coming."

Gracie giggled and Ian listened with half an ear, thinking how grand it would be if his father could be around to put him to bed once in a blue moon at least.

"What's a blue moon?" Daniel asked.

Ian wanted to crawl under the covers and hide. He hadn't meant to speak his wish aloud. It was bad enough having divorced parents when these kids had such a super life with theirs. He didn't need them feeling sorry for him. He looked about the room and realized that at least Mr. Osborne had gone and hadn't heard. That was something anyway.

"It means not often but at least sometimes," Ian answered impatiently trying not to show his embarrassment.

"Then why didn't you just say that?" Daniel grumbled. "I have to put up with this old saying stuff from big people. I shouldn't have to put up with it from a kid. I mean, what's a blue moon, anyway? I never saw the moon look blue."

"Oh, Daniel," Rachel whispered, "Ian's from another country. He's always going to talk different. Don't bug him the way you do everyone else. Besides, he has enough problems with his parents being divorced. He doesn't need you getting on his nerves. And don't say it. You know what getting on someone's nerves is. You do it all the time!"

"Is it awful being a divorced kid?" Mickey asked.

Ian sighed. These were his new mates. Maybe it wouldn't hurt to tell them how he was feeling. "It's always been just Mum and me. My dad has never put me to bed. Not once in my whole life. When we lived in Paris and London, I could pretend that it was because he was an American and lived so far away. But now he's not far at all. And I know him now, so I know what I'm missing."

"They should both live with you," Daniel decreed.

"They're divorced, Daniel," Rachel said. "You remember before our Mommy and Daddy died in the accident? Uncle Trent and Aunt Maggie didn't live together. That was because they were getting divorced so they couldn't live together anymore.''

"Then maybe Pastor Jim and your mom should get married again," Grace said simply. "That way he could live with you and your mom."

"I think my dad still loves Mum but she was really angry when she first saw him again. I don't know if she'd marry him."

Mickey sat up and turned toward the others. "I think Gracie's right, anyway."

"Course I am," Gracie said. "What am I right about?"

"That they need to get married again," Mickey answered. "It's good that one of them still loves the other one. Mom loved Dad before he lived with us. Whenever he called to talk to me in the hospital in Florida, she always sort of got this dreamy sad look. Just like Pastor Jim gets when your Mom's around, Ian. We need them to be around each other and get used to each other again."

Daniel sat up now. "That way they won't get on each other's nerves when they get married and live together again. Remember when Uncle Trent stayed in the carriage house? He said adults get on each other's nerves if they're stuck together too much all of a sudden."

"But Dad is really busy with the church," Ian protested as he too sat up, feeling as if he were watching a tennis match.

"Then we'll have to help them," Rachel decided.

"I've got it," Mickey exclaimed. "Tomorrow you were supposed to come to church with us, Ian. I think you should tell your mom you want her to come, too. Make a real big deal out of the Fourth of July celebration afterward. That's a start. We'll think of other stuff to do later. We need to have regular meetings at the tree house. And Gracie, it's a Kids' Club Secret. You know what that means."

Ian saw Gracie nod vigorously in the dark. "That if I tell I'm in trouble with a cap-it-able *T* and not part of the club anymore."

"What do we call our battle plan?" Rachel asked, scratching her head.

"Operation Wedding Ring," Mickey declared. "Secret?"

"Secret," each of his new mates repeated as a promise and so he too said, "Secret," and felt just a little more in control—a little more hopeful. It was going to work out. They were going to fix it!

Holly woke to incessant knocking at her door. She jumped out of bed, her heart pounding. Her first thought was that something was wrong with Ian. As she tore through the small apartment, the brilliant sunlight registered in her sleepy brain about the same time she realized that Trent and Maggie would have called and not taken the time to run across the yard to tell her. And since Ian was next door, it shouldn't be the Osborne kids knocking up for him again. And it wasn't. It was Ian.

"Mum! You aren't ready! Hurry. You'll be late for services."

"I'm not going today. That's why you stayed with the Osbornes."

Ian looked positively horrified. "But you and I always go to Sunday church together. I told them that. They left already. There wouldn't have been room in their van for both of us and the grandmothers. They stayed last night, too. Please, Mum. It's their Independence Day. There's to be a huge church barbecue afterward with lots of games and prizes. And movies and crafts. You have to be there. Please. I don't want to miss it. I was ever so certain you'd want to go."

This was exactly what Holly had feared. And there seemed no way out. Ian would clearly be crushed were he to miss this. "Very well. But Ian, you must understand that this could be quite awkward for me. I'm the pastor's ex-wife. People frown on divorce in the church."

"Oh. We—*I* hadn't thought. It's okay. I don't need to go." Ian's crestfallen expression as he turned away nearly broke her heart.

"I'll be ready in just a few minutes. We may be a bit late but perhaps that's just as well. I can slip into the sanctuary more easily this way."

Ian smiled. "Thanks, Mum. You won't be sorry. I promise."

As Holly parked her car about the same place she'd sat and listened to Jim tell of the start of the church, she wasn't so sure of Ian's promise. She was still attracted to Jim. And that frightened her. Her feelings and emotions were mixed up and she didn't know which way to turn. The more she learned of the man, the more she realized that she'd loved someone else entirely. The scary part was that *this* Jim was even more compelling than the man she'd met nine years ago.

And what of that other man—the man she'd cast out of her life and heart? a voice deep inside her asked. Where was he? Was he still part of this new Jim? Would he once again surface like a monster from the deep or was he banished forever?

Holly slipped into the back of the church as the band struck up a lively tune. There were two men and three women on a raised platform on either side of the podium who were singing. Behind them were a two guitarists, a drummer and a keyboard player. It was like no church orchestra she'd ever seen.

And Jim wasn't up there yet. Odd though this church seemed, the hymn being sung reached into Holly and soothed her soul. She felt a sense of peace descend on her and everyone around her raised their hands to the Lord in praise.

After the song ended one of the men stepped forward to pray for the country and for the wisdom of its leaders. Then the band played "God Bless America" and everyone joyfully joined in on the patriotic hymn. The sweet sound rose to the rafters and Holly was sure the notes floated far beyond and that the angels in heaven had joined in. During the song Jim walked forward and loped up the steps. He looked just as relaxed as if he were ascending Trent and

Maggie's back porch. She was surprised that he wore a pair of jeans and a navy-blue golf shirt.

"Good morning, everyone," he called out when the congregation sat at the end of the song.

Everyone called back, "Good morning!"

"I bumped into Ted and Jean Jensen at the grocery store a couple weeks ago. Most of you probably know them. They run the Sunday school. We got to talking there in the aisle about the way it is here. Somewhere in the conversation one or the other of us mentioned the Lord's sheep.

"When I came in last night I checked the messages on the machine. There was one from our township commissioner. I since learned that our innocent conversation at the GoGo Mart had sparked quite a controversy. I've straightened out the problem but I just had to share his message with all of you. I wrote it down so you'd get it word for word." He pulled a piece of paper out of his Bible.

"'Okay, Dillon. I went to bat for you. We rezoned that land so you bunch of crazy Christians could wear jeans and go to church in a barn. But you can't have it both ways. You've got to get rid of the sheep!'"

Holly had never heard such laughter in her father's church but when the congregation quieted, Jim didn't keep them rolling in the aisles. That apparently wasn't his style.

"I wonder how many of us ever stop to think how lucky we are. We can gather in a place like this where we can wear jeans or suits or whatever we feel is appropriate. We can sing songs and pray without fear.

We can only imagine what it must be like to live where this kind of gathering could mean death.

"Some of our founding fathers knew. And when a subsequent generation broke with England they knew that it would always be a possibility when men intrude in the affairs of God. They fought a long bloody war to ensure our ability to live and worship as we see fit and later tried to protect that right with our remarkable constitution.

"Today we honor those men and the freedoms they assured us. But I can't help but wonder what we'd do if we had to make the same kinds of tough decisions that our forefathers did. Would our children and our children's children be as free as we are today? Would we risk our homes and fortunes? Our big-screen TVs and SUVs?"

Holly looked around at the congregation as most chuckled at Jim's last remark. He commanded their attention as her father never had. No one squirmed. No one nodded off. Every now and then he'd crack another joke and they'd all laugh. Then he'd follow it up with a truth so poignant it would bring tears to the eye. He spoke of faith and the many impossible victories during the revolution that God had granted the rebels.

He cited scripture verses and gave witty pointers where they could be found, telling those new to the Bible to turn left or right from their present location. People chuckled, learned their Bible better and a few shouted "Amen" or "Praise God" when he said something that touched their hearts. And he touched many.

Why couldn't he have been this Jim when we were married, Lord? Why couldn't You have called him to You sooner? Why couldn't he have sought You out instead of seeking out every pub in a five-mile radius of our flat?

Her father came to her mind again, then came memories of nights spent alone at Ian's side in hospitals all over the world. The sight of Alan and Christie still and cold in their coffins slammed into her. She'd wanted Jim at her side that day but he'd been gone by then. It had taken months for her to stop listening and hoping to hear his little car pulling up outside.

Holly was suddenly rigid with anger. Anger at Jim. Anger at herself. Anger at her father and, worst of all, anger at God. She stood before she even realized her intent. And Jim's gaze collided with hers over the heads of the congregation. He stopped midsentence and stared at her. Holly couldn't handle the confusion she saw on his face and turned away, nearly diving for the nearby door.

In her wake, she left an awful silence. Even in her agitation she knew her sudden exit had probably rattled Jim past the ability to recover. But she couldn't help that now. Flight was all she could think of.

Holly was sure that Trent and Maggie would look after Ian so Holly headed for her car only to realize that she'd left her purse and keys behind. She turned back but Jim had apparently brought the service to a quick conclusion. The congregation began to filter out and she just couldn't face them.

The sunlight was blinding so Holly stepped around the corner into the shadow of the building and behind the seclusion of an ornamental cedar. She stood there for a few minutes wishing she had remembered her purse when she heard some church members pass, questioning their pastor's sudden distraction. Others who had seen her abrupt exit had correctly concluded that she was the ex-wife their pastor had told them about recently.

"How sad when love isn't enough to pull people through troubled times," one woman said, her voice fading as she moved away toward her car.

Holly was mortified. She hastened to the back of the barn and in the distance she saw the old timber frame derelict Jim had spoken of the day before. At that moment it looked like a haven. She'd almost reached it when she heard her name called. Holly turned to see that Maggie had followed her.

"Want to talk?" Maggie asked when she caught up.

Holly shrugged. "I'm not sure there's anything to talk about."

"How about a thoroughly disconcerted man who, for the first time, just flubbed his sermon?"

"I'm sorry about that," she said and stepped into the building that Jim was so intent on saving. It smelled of rot and decay. She didn't see the attraction except that it wasn't the church. "I just had to get out of there. I knew it would be a mistake to come here today, but I let Ian talk me into it. There's still so much anger in me toward Jim, Maggie. All I could think watching him was, why couldn't he have changed for me? Why couldn't he have stopped drinking before he destroyed our marriage?''

"He didn't reform on his own. The Lord worked in his life. You know that. He's never taken a lick of credit for where he is today.''

"I know that. How about this, then? Why now when it's too late?''

"Is it too late? What's too late, Holly? Too late is when one of you is dead. Believe me. Trent and I were waiting for our divorce to be finalized when Michael and Sarah were killed and left the children in our care. There were very bitter feelings on both sides but with the Lord's help we got past all of that to the love we both still felt deep in out hearts.''

Holly clutched her hands tightly. "I'm not sure there's love for him still in me. He killed it. There are all these memories to contend with. It would be so much simpler if I could just wipe out the past and forget. I look at him now and I don't want to remember him sitting on the settee drinking until he passed out. I don't want to remember the nights he never came home. I want to forget that he wasn't with me when Ian was born. Did you know that? I just wanted him to hold my hand and he wasn't there!''

Maggie took her stiff hands in hers. "You couldn't still feel this much anger if you didn't still care a great deal for him.''

"I don't know about that. When I talk to him, I

can't find the man I met and loved. I can't even confront the man who disappeared from my life and didn't try to patch up our marriage. He doesn't seem to exist any longer. Pastor Jim Dillon is nothing like him. Last night he even admitted that he pretended to be someone he wasn't to win me. So, who was he really then? And who is he now?''

"How do you feel about the man he is now?"

"I'd be lying if I said I wasn't attracted to him. Or that I didn't admire him. Because I am and I do."

"How do you feel about him being in Ian's life?"

"Afraid. What if the other Jim surfaces? Ian could be hurt. Then there's the man I'm coming to know. He'd be a good father for Ian. I know my son needs a man's guidance but how do I trust a man who seems to be a chameleon?"

Maggie turned when footsteps approached. "One day at a time. One step at a time. But Holly, you have to try. You owe it to all three of you. Maybe you need to say the things to Jim you just said to me. He needs to answer for the things that still have you so angry. And you need to forgive him or you'll never be able to get beyond your past."

Just then Jim stepped through an opening in one of the precarious walls. "I think we should talk, Holly. Do you mind, Maggie?"

"Not at all. I was about to suggest it. We'll help get the setup for today organized. You worry about yourself for a change."

After Maggie left, silence reigned. Holly didn't know where to begin or what she was ready to reveal.

She looked up at him finally as the silence began to stretch her nerves.

"Was it something I said?" he quipped with a grin that she knew was forced. "You really hated my analogy of the Jews winning the promised land and the rebels securing freedom from England?"

She smiled sadly. He had such a sharp wit. That about him was the same. "I just got so angry. I had to get out of there. I'm sorry I threw you off your stride and embarrassed you."

He shrugged. "Jesus hung naked on a cross before a whole city. I can take messing up a sermon now and again. And they're a forgiving bunch. I'm much more concerned about you. You said you were angry. At anyone besides me?"

"You, my father, God, me, even Ian a little I guess."

"So pull up a log and start with the simplest anger to explain. You have to talk it out or it's going to fester and destroy you."

Holly noticed a beam that had been fashioned into some sort of temporary seating. She sank down on it carefully and Jim straddled it to face her. "Ian's the simplest I guess. I've been his whole world and he mine. I'm the one who walked the floors when he had fevers and rushed him to hospitals in the middle of the night, and scrimped and saved so he could have the things he needed. Now you come into his life and you're the great big hero. And me? Lately, I'm just old can-you-make-us-lunch-Mum, why-can't-I-go-Mum, you're-mean-Mum."

"I guess I could yell at him for something but—"

"Don't make light of it!" she shouted and blinked back angry tears. "It hurts when he says I should have stayed married to you. I was only trying to protect him!"

"And you did," Jim said quietly and took her hand. "You'll never know how grateful I am that you did. I'll talk to him, and explain about what a mess I was and I'll tell him how badly his attitude is hurting you. He loves you, Holly."

Holly nodded. She knew Ian loved her, and with the way Jim was looking at her she suspected that he did, as well. That hurt, too, and made her furious and glad all at once.

"Now who else were you angry with?" he asked.

"My father. He was supposed to be a man of God. How could he be the way he was and read the Word every day? No sermon he ever gave touched hearts the way yours did. I feel doubly betrayed. He was a failure as a father and a pastor."

"That I *can* answer because I've spent time with your father. The gospel never touched his heart. It's like Jesus said in Matthew, 'Many will say to Me in that day, Lord, Lord, have we not prophesied in Your name, cast out demons in Your name, and done many wonders in Your name? And then I will declare to them, I never knew you; depart from Me.' That's because they never knew *Him*. But your father does know Him now. The Lord has changed George's life as much as He has mine. So does that bring us to your anger at yourself, me or God?"

Holly pulled her hand away and stood. She could feel the agitation rushing back. She took a calming breath and plunged on. They had to get all this out in the open. Maggie was right. "Maybe all of the above. I can't deny the changes I see in you, but why couldn't He have changed you when *I* needed you."

"I can't answer that. It's my own daily question to Him, too. I'll tell you what answers He's given me about it so far. His name in those days was nothing more than a swear word to me. I didn't know Him or seek Him so He wouldn't change me. *I* had to turn to God. It doesn't work the other way around. *He* knocks but *we* have to answer. I guess I just didn't hear Him."

Holly thought that was about as good an answer as either of them were likely to get. "I guess I'm next," she said and sighed. "*I* knew He was out there knocking. Why didn't I tell you about Him. Why didn't I tell you He could help you?"

"Did you know He could help? Did you even know Him? Really know Him—the way you do now? His name was more than a curse to you, to be sure. But because you never took His name in vain and you attended your father's church every Sunday, did that help you? You just got done telling me that George failed you as a pastor. Don't you know the Lord *now* in a way that you didn't *then?*"

"Well, yes. That came later in Sydney," Holly admitted and thought she understood what he was saying but not completely. "But why didn't I do more to help you than just demand you change? Why didn't I, at least, call your commanding officer?''

Jim looked troubled and deep in thought. ''I wouldn't have thanked you for it. I know that much. And I doubt he would have done much anyway. Unless I got hurt or hurt someone else, he would have seen you as the daughter of a minister who didn't like my social drinking. Holly, we talked about this. Stop second-guessing what you did in the past. I'm not in the least angry with you.''

''You were. That day in my apartment you were angry that I'd kept you from Ian.''

''And now I'm not. If there was any wrong done on your part, I forgive you and I understand why you felt you had to disappear.''

Well, that tore it! ''I didn't disappear!'' she screamed at him. ''You did. You left the flat before Ian even came home from hospital after the asthma attack. You'd cleared out your clothes and were gone. I heard you'd deployed to the Operation Deep Freeze base and you'd never even come to see how Ian was.''

Jim looked confused. ''I did what you asked.''

All the years of fear and worry seemed to coalesce inside her and explode as anger. ''Do you know how afraid I was when I had to deliver him among strangers? I'd alienated my parents for you, and you let me deliver with only strange sisters and doctors to comfort me. And do you have any idea how frightened I was that night when Ian couldn't breathe? He was so tiny and nothing I did helped. I needed you and you weren't there. So when you came at last, I said the only thing I thought might shock you into changing. Instead, as if I'd handed you a prize you'd been seeking, you took your freedom and never looked back.''

"Never looked back? That's what you think?"

Holly dashed away the flow of tears that had begun to blur her vision but they came right back. "I know you had a change of heart after finding the Lord and getting sober. But before that? Yes!" she cried on a racking sob, "that's exactly what I think!"

Chapter Ten

Jim felt as if his heart were being torn in two as Holly screamed her anger and cried out her pain. It was clear there was little hope for them, but she needed to understand how he'd gotten where he had. And how much losing her had meant to him even within a cloud of alcohol-induced delirium. He looked up into her tear-filled eyes then away, hating the hurt he'd inflicted on her. He focused on the ground.

"You couldn't be more wrong, Holly. You were my dream come true. Something unspoiled and clean in my life. I knew before I even had you that I'd lose you eventually. It was the pattern of my life. I cared for someone and they left or I had to leave. My father, my sister, my foster family, my mother. Life taught me young that love doesn't last. Every minute I was with you, I knew it would end. I tried to run from the pain of losing you and all I did was push you away in the process. The tragedy is that I made it happen. A self-fulfilling prophecy.

"After I packed up my clothes that morning you asked for the divorce, I went to a friend's flat on the other side of Christchurch. I don't remember anything about that next week. I woke up strapped into the belly of a C130 on my way to the Deep Freeze installation. Once we got there, I found out there was rarely anything to do but drink, which suited me just fine. I think I stayed drunk for the whole six months we were there. Then I came back to divorce papers.

"That's when I figured out what I was going to do. I was going to kill myself. It seemed like the only way to end the pain of this yawning hole inside me that losing you and Ian had caused."

Holly had her back to him but he looked up in time to see her stiffen. He didn't want to cause her more pain than he already had, but he also knew she needed to hear all of it. "Sure, I signed the divorce papers without even reading them. I wasn't supposed to be alive much longer so it didn't matter what they said. To me, the divorce meant you wouldn't have to pay to bury me. But I couldn't seem to do it. I like to think the Lord protected me from myself.

"My next duty station was stateside here in Philadelphia. A year later the navy and I parted company. Happily, on their part. From the time I heard Mrs. Dunbar, my foster mother, and her kids talk about her husband, joining the navy was what I wanted. And drinking caused me to lose that, as well. That's when it got really bad. I sold everything I owned for booze and started living on the streets in Riverside.

"It was six months after that when I heard about a mission where I could get a meal and a warm bed for at least one night. But I got more than that. The price was taking a shower, putting on the clean clothes they gave me and staying for the service. I thought Angel Peterson, the woman who ran the place, was a fool. It didn't seem like an even trade to me so I went along to get the meal figuring I'd sleep through the service.

"The guy preaching that night was Greg Peterson, Angel's husband. I didn't sleep. He talked about salvation in a way that cut through the rhetoric of religion and right to the personal level. Me. God. Salvation. After he gave the altar call, he started singing, 'Come Just as You Are.' And I got up and walked forward. He'd promised healing and I didn't figure there was a person alive who needed that more than I did."

He felt Holly move closer but didn't look up. He just kept going, driven by the need to share the most important event in his life with her. "Greg put me to work at the mission and he worked by my side. I knew he wanted me to talk about myself, but I was afraid to look back. I was afraid if I did I'd drink again or just outright commit suicide."

Holly's sob almost stopped him but Jim pressed on. Something told him that unless she understood where he'd been, she couldn't really know how much their divorce had cost him or understand how much he'd learned to depend on the Lord. "Greg used to be a cop," he continued, "and I guess it taught him patience because day after day he just waited for me to open up. He's the most patient guy I've ever met. The night his wife had their first child—a boy—I broke down and cried like a baby. It brought all I'd destroyed into such sharp focus. He had what I could have had, but I'd thrown it all away. I told him about my childhood and about you and Ian."

Now he looked up into her tear-stained face, his own tears trailing down his cheeks. "After that I started looking for you and healing. But I still cry myself to sleep some nights because of all I've lost. No, Holly, far from prizing my freedom, I've hated every day of it."

"Oh, I was so wrong!" she sobbed. "I've blamed you for all of it and I failed you as much as you failed me."

"No!" Jim cried and sprang to his feet. Her sobbing increased and in desperation he took her in his arms, hoping to offer comfort. *Astonishment* was too tame a word to express his feelings when she seemed to burrow closer into his embrace. He rocked her and whispered calming words, telling her he had been wrong from the start. That he was the one who'd never given them a chance. That she'd done the only thing she could do.

As his own tears dried against her silky hair, Jim felt her relax in his arms. Her weeping slowed and the sobs that had racked her slim body subsided.

And that was when Jim grew increasingly aware of

a more dangerous need than the need to comfort her. He realized that he'd waded into treacherous waters, so he took her shoulders to set her away. But Holly looked up at him, her eyes like liquid emeralds, her lips begging to be kissed. Good intentions and even better sense flew out the nonexistent windows of the tumbling building. He bent his head to cover her sweet mouth with his.

Like a jolt of electricity the kiss jangled his nerve endings. Like a bolt of lightning it set fire to his every cell. The air rushed from his lungs. Jim broke the kiss. Gasping for air and sanity, he released her.

But the connection between them was not so easily broken. Their gazes seemed to stay as entwined as their arms had been moments before. Jim swallowed, still caught in the snare of those electric green eyes of hers.

"I don't think I'll apologize for that this time," he confessed slowly.

Holly, green eyes wide and dazed, said, "I...uh...I don't think...I want one."

"I'm glad you feel that way, but I don't think I'd better do it again, either."

"No. That might not be such a good idea," Holly agreed, still looking as shell-shocked as he felt.

"And I think maybe we both have a lot of thinking to do about where this is leading. I don't know what losing you again would do to me if I start thinking we may have a future and then you decide you still can't trust me."

Holly nodded. "You're right. I need to find that

trust before we can even think farther than week to week.''

"Is there a chance do you think? Even a slim one that there's hope for us to be together?" Jim held his breath, waiting for her answer. Praying it would be the one he needed to hear.

Holly nodded, smiling shyly, and Jim couldn't resist another quick hug. "Thank you," he whispered against her hair. "I'll prove I'm worthy of another chance. I promise."

"Mum. Dad. Is everything all right?" Ian asked from just outside the building.

They broke apart guiltily and Jim cleared his throat. "Everything's just fine. Stay outside. This place is a little dangerous."

"Then how come you and Mum are in there?"

"We're coming out, Ian," Holly said and rolled her eyes. "Now I'll get a safety lecture. So, tell me about this church picnic."

The day was perfect if a little hot. Games for children and adults had been organized. Holly felt a little awkward at first, but the Osborne clan rallied around her, and she soon relaxed. She even entered a water balloon toss with Jim and laughed with the others when he caught it with his arms high in the air and got an impromptu shower. Ever the good sport, Jim laughed hardest as he shook his head and sent a spray of water flying from his hair.

She met a few of Jim's friends, the most memorable of whom were the Petersons, the couple who had been so instrumental in Jim's salvation. Angelica Peterson was a small redhead expecting her third child, a girl for her daddy to spoil this time, she told Holly. Greg was tall and powerfully built and not at all what Holly had expected. Jim had said Peterson was once a police officer and this was easier to believe than that he was a minister of God. That was until Greg Peterson put his two-year-old son on his shoulders. The towheaded toddler took hold of his father's blond hair and his proud father's blue eyes sparkled with a touchingly gentle love.

Mealtime arrived and, just as it had at Maggie and Trent's the day before, the same curious behavior concerning Jim and his meal occurred again. All the women fussed and fluttered around him until his plate sagged under the weight of his food. Ian needed help just as Holly was about to ask Maggie why they were all so concerned about Jim's diet.

As the sun set, volunteers herded the children into the sanctuary for a movie while outside, the church's many musicians took turns singing praise songs around a bonfire. They were all talented and clearly the spirit of God inspired each of them, but then Greg Peterson took a guitar from Jim's outstretched hand and began playing a sweet melody.

Jim stood to address the gathering. "I know most of you but there are some faces here I don't recognize. I have a feeling that one or two of you are sitting there thinking, 'Oh no, here it comes. I let Aunt Hattie or cousin Milton or my friend Calvin drag me here for a free meal and now I have to pay by listening to the preacher man.' Well hey, you know the old saying—there's no such thing as a free lunch!''

Holly giggled along with just about everyone and then Jim continued to talk in a quiet, campfire tone about the joy, peace, forgiveness and love of Christ. He told much the same story about his own life and conversion to Christianity that he'd told her, skimming over some of the parts that were clearly too personal and painful for him to share with strangers.

He talked for about ten minutes sharing the love and forgiveness of Christ. And finally about the recent loss of one of their founding members. ''This week the folks here at the Tabernacle buried a brother. Jake Testa was never sick a day in his life and then two years ago—Bam. One heart attack after another. In the end Jake knew his life here was over. He said something to me that last night that I think defined the man and his faith.

'''Jim,' he said, 'would you look at all these bozos trying anything they can to keep my heart beating? They don't get it. Death isn't optional.' Jake slipped away after that and went home to be with the Lord. If you're here tonight, and you don't know where you'd go if you didn't open your eyes tomorrow, then maybe there's a bigger reason than a free meal that brought you here.

''I was talking to a special person in my life earlier today and I said that Jesus is always knocking on the door of men's hearts but that each man needs to answer. He's knocking on *your* door tonight. He's asking you to invite Him into your heart. Into your life. He won't come in uninvited. But He will come in."

Jim stopped talking and let that sweet tune that floated from Greg Peterson's guitar fill the air until Jim asked anyone wanting to open the door to Jesus and salvation to come forward. At that point Peterson's even sweeter tenor voice joined the strains of the tune singing, "Come Just as You Are," the tune Jim said had accompanied him on his own walk forward toward salvation.

Holly felt tears well up as one after another five people got up from the ground and walked forward. Jim led them in prayer and then they were swamped by joyful family and friends who'd brought them.

Minutes later she realized that people had begun to drift away to their cars or to the church to pick up their children. Holly stayed where she was, watching the flames of the bonfire tame to embers. The day had turned out to be a small miracle and she didn't want it to end.

"Penny for your thoughts," Jim said some time later.

Holly looked up and chuckled. "I'm not sure I have any. I've just been sitting here letting my mind drift nowhere. That was beautiful. You and your friend make quite a team."

"Oh, he doesn't need me. If he'd been speaking, there'd have been a stampede to the front."

"You, sir, are too modest. What you've built here is incredible."

Jim shook his head and sat down next to her. "I

haven't done a thing. It's all the spirit of God. If He moves in a church, this is the result.''

Holly wasn't convinced but she had a more important matter to discuss. It was an idea she'd toyed with on and off all day. "Hmm. If you say so. Jim? Where do you live?''

Jim felt his stomach turn to a rock. Where did he live? No place he could house a wife and child. "In a—a couple rooms at the back of the church.'' Why hadn't he thought of this before asking for another chance with her? "I haven't needed much space. Why?''

"I received a call from the ambassador late Friday. I was able to delegate most of my current projects before I left New York, but there are some rather sensitive negotiations later this week that he needs me to handle. I'd planned to either take Ian back with me or leave him with Maggie and Trent. But now I wonder if you'd like to have him with you. Have you room for him, do you think?''

"Oh, sure. I can put him up with no trouble,'' he said mentally rearranging his meager living space. "That would be great. Does Ian know?''

Holly chuckled. "Do you think if I'd mentioned the possibility to him that he wouldn't have been bouncing all over the place all day?''

"Guess not. When would you leave?''

"I think if I leave Wednesday I can take care of everything for the meeting on Friday but I might stay a bit longer. We agreed that I need to think, and I've decided I can't do that around you or Ian. This isn't about you and him. You're his father and I won't stop you from seeing him as long as I believe he's safe with you. This is about us, and I need to consider just us in the equation. And I need to be alone to do that.''

"Look at them," Ian said, as he and the oldest two members of the Kids' Club peeked out of a second-story classroom window of the Tabernacle.

"Isn't it romantic?" Rachel sighed.

"You should have seen the way he kissed her this afternoon. Now *that* was romantic.''

"He kissed her today?" Mickey asked, his eyes bulging.

"Oh, did he ever. And the best part was she didn't yell at him. I couldn't hear what they said afterward, but Mum chuckled as they came outside, so she couldn't have been angry."

"So I guess that's it for our job. This is the shortest mission we've ever had," Rachel said. "Our last mission lasted nearly two years before we got Grace her kitty. This was so easy."

Mickey shook his head and crossed his arms. "Mom was a tougher case than we originally thought, and I'm not convinced this is as easy as it looks, either. They're talking and kissing. That just isn't enough. We need make sure there's a wedding. Ian doesn't need parents who just kiss each other. He needs ones who live together."

"Then what do we do next?" Ian asked.

"I suppose you keep making sure they have to be together. Get them to do stuff with you."

"I don't know," Rachel countered, her eyes narrowed as if she were squinting, trying to see something out of place and far away.

Rachel was right. There was something wrong with Mickey's plan. And, when Ian thought about all that had happened that day, he realized what it was. "As soon as they knew I was there, Dad and Mum jumped apart. And did you notice that they hardly even talked to each other all day till now when they're alone?"

"So then we need to make sure they're alone with each other as much as possible," Mickey said.

Rachel sighed and plopped down on a big pillow. "This is going to be harder than the kitten. That's for sure."

"Not if we really analyze this," Mickey said wisely. Mickey was about the smartest boy Ian had ever met. Oh, he wasn't all that good at the things Ian was, like computers and math, but he had a keen mind and could figure out all sorts of ways to do things. "Where is Pastor Jim most of the time?"

"Here," both Ian and Rachel answered at once.

"Right. And Mrs. Dillon is at our place. If we break something at the carriage house, Dad will just fix it. But, if Pastor Jim needed your Mum's help, she'd have to come here where he always is. What's your Mum good at? Besides cooking. Everyone feeds your dad already, so that won't do."

"Well, she cleans really well."

"So does Pastor Jim."

"What's she do in New York? You know for a job?"

"Oh, she's a trade specialist. I don't see dad needing that. She's a whiz at typing and making graphs on the computer, too. And math."

Rachel and Mickey stared at each other. "Mrs. White!" Rachel announced. "She'll help. I heard Mom say she's the worst of the matchmakers."

"Matchmakers?" Ian didn't like the sounds of that. "Isn't that someone who gets dates for other people? My mum called her boss that once when he got her a date for a party."

"The ladies are always trying to get your dad dates. He hates it. Let's go see if Mrs. White could be sick or something for a week or two," Mickey suggested. "If she couldn't be in the office, maybe your mom would help out. Then they'd be at the church during the days when hardly nobody else is there. Or maybe Mrs. White could think of something even more clever."

"Why would she help?"

Rachel smiled. "Oh, she'd do anything for us. She used to be our baby-sitter and she helped Mom with the house. She lived in the carriage house before you and your mom. When Daniel and Gracie weren't so hard to take care of anymore, she started helping your dad with the office at the church. Let's go ask her to join Operation Wedding Ring."

Chapter Eleven

Confounded, Holly stared across the settee at Ian as he gaped at her. His expression had her wanting to check the mirror to see if she had indeed grown a second head. Both she and Jim had thought he'd be thrilled with the news that he'd be staying at the Tabernacle.

"You're going back to New York?" he asked uncertainly.

"That's what I said. And you'll be staying with your dad till I get back," she responded as casually as she could, considering how confused she was by his reaction. What was the problem here?

"And you'll be gone for a week?" Ian asked, now clearly worried and actually wringing his hands.

There was something definitely wrong here. *Oh, please don't let it be that Jim was drinking on the sly.* "Possibly less but no more than that. Poppet, what is it? Weren't you comfortable at your father's last night? Did something happen to upset you?''

"It was fine. Dad was great."

Holly breathed a mental sigh of relief when a possible explanation occurred to her. "If you're worried about your asthma, don't. We have it all covered. If Dad's needed when Mrs. White isn't at the church, he'll bring you to stay with the Osbornes. Everyone knows what to do for you in case of an attack."

"It isn't that. Dad can handle anything. I just don't think you should be away from home right now."

"Dear, our being in Pennsylvania *is* away from home. New York is home for now till I'm assigned elsewhere. Have you forgotten our flat in Peter Cooper Village? Renting this lovely place is only temporary."

Ian looked away. "No. I haven't forgotten."

The gloomy tone of his voice twisted Holly's heart. She reached out, untangled his twisting fingers and held both his hands in hers. "What is it? Talk to me, Ian. I can't help if I don't know what it is that has you so troubled."

Ian pulled his hands away and crossed his arms slumping into the cushions in a classic pouting position. "I don't want to go back there. Ever. I like it here. I like being so near my dad. I know you aren't fond of your father but at least you had one. I finally do and I don't want to only see him once a month if I'm lucky. That's how it is for Joey Taylor because he lives so far from his father. Why can't we live permanently near to Dad?"

"Oh, poppet. I don't have my job as a lark. It supports us. And New York is where I work. Even if I could get another job down here, I'm in this country as a diplomat. I can't just decide to stay indefinitely and change positions. It isn't a decision I can make willy-nilly."

Ian's expression turned mutinous. "Is there no way, or is it just that you don't want me to be near Dad?" he shouted. "You divorced him to keep me from having a father and now you're still trying to mess it up after I finally found him!"

Holly sucked a shocked breath at her son's sudden attack but it was Jim who countered the remark. "*That* was unfair, Ian," he growled through the screen door behind them.

He'd brought Ian home and was working on a problem over at Trent and Maggie's so his appearance wasn't a surprise, but the tone he spoke to Ian in certainly was. And it was a welcome one.

"Come in and join the discussion," she said as Ian jumped up from the settee and turned around to stare in horrified fascination at Jim as he came in and rounded the furniture grouping.

Jim looked down at her and she could see an apology in his eyes. "Would you mind if I addressed his remarks?"

"Be my guest," she invited, motioning him to the big overstuffed chair near the hearth.

After sitting, Jim gestured for Ian to sit down as well. No doubt her son already regretted his outburst. Jim seemed displeased and quite formidable.

"Everything your mother has done in these past eight years has been for you. When she asked for a divorce, she had every reason in the world to do it. You were a baby, Son. You don't know what I was like in those days. I was stupid and irresponsible. It would have been easier for her to just stay with me and let me support her financially but she cared what kind of influence a drunk would have on your life. She did what she did to protect you, and I for one am grateful she did it. If she hadn't, I might have disappointed you in a thousand ways by now, and you'd want to live as far from me as you could."

"I'm sorry," Ian said, casting his teary eyes toward Jim.

"Don't apologize to *me*. It was your mother you hurt by shouting at her and treating her so badly. Apologize to *her*."

Ian turned in his seat to face her fully. His tears flowed freely and his lower lip quivered. "I'm sorry for what I said, Mum."

"And how about for shouting at her?" Jim coaxed sternly.

"And—and for shouting. I'm sorry, Mum."

Holly put her arms out when Ian's face crumpled and he dove into her arms, sobbing. Jim stood. He looked as torn up as Ian, and a lot more uncertain. She held out her hand to him. It couldn't be easy to suddenly be a father and to have to discipline your child when you were still just getting to know him.

"Thank you," she mouthed and squeezed his hand. He nodded, motioning himself to the door with a question in his eyes. Holly didn't know if he should leave or not. Everything in both their lives was suddenly uncertain. But Ian had wanted his father around more and being told by Jim that he'd misbehaved would be part of it. Had they been a real family, Jim wouldn't be expected to leave just because Ian was upset with him. She shook her head and mouthed, "Stay."

Holly gave Ian one last squeeze with her free arm and he squirmed away. "Suppose you go wash your face and then make a list of things to take to Dad's."

Ian nodded and left with his head down.

Jim grimaced. "Holly, he didn't even look at me."

She realized she still held his hand, so she pulled him down next to her where Ian had been seated. He slouched gratefully down next to her. "He's not going to stop loving you just because you chastised him any more than you love him less because he made you angry," she told him.

"He made me angry because I could see you flinch when he shouted at you. You've been hurt enough by me without Ian hurting you because of me."

"I think he got that message loud and clear. You did that very well. Where did you learn to be a father when you hardly remember your own?"

"I had a Father. My Father in heaven. I just didn't know it. Reading His Word seems to prepare us for all the roles we play in life. And I've watched other men, of course. Jake with his son. Trent with the tribe."

Holly wondered if he'd learned as much about being a husband. And then she wondered if she'd ever have the nerve to find out. She was beginning to hope she would. Perhaps it was time she began praying she would.

"So, what brings you by? Did you want to see Ian?"

Jim's gaze seemed to caress her face. "I just spent the night with Ian. I wanted to see you."

Holly felt a blush heat her cheeks. "Why?"

"Because I love looking at you, being with you." His eyes sparkled but then he sighed and wiped a hand over his face. "And because I wondered if you could help me out when you get back. Mrs. White has been a great hand at the church in the office, but she isn't doing so good with the bookkeeping. In fact, she's got it in such a tangle I can't figure out how to get it right. Trent just failed miserably, too. I thought he was my last hope. Then Mickey said that Ian was bragging about what a whiz you are with math."

"I could look at it now."

Jim groaned. "Not now. I'd rather face a firing squad than all those figures again. My head's throbbing."

"Don't you have a treasurer?"

Jim's chuckle was full of pain. "Jake Testa."

"Oh, Jim. I'm so sorry. I'll bet everyone forgets that you lost a friend, not just a church elder."

"The only memorial service I've ever done that was harder was for Michael and Sarah Osborne. Mike had become a close friend and, yeah, I wound up comforting everyone else that time, too."

He closed his eyes and Holly thought she'd never seen a grown man more in need of comfort. It occurred to her that except for his time with her he might never have had anyone offer him even a simple hug, and she wanted to give him at least that. She knelt up next to him, kissed his forehead and cradled his head against her. In turn Jim wrapped his arms about her waist.

Jim just about melted against Holly when she reached out and held him. This was the one thing missing in his life. A helpmate. Someone who cared. Someone he could talk to. Someone to love. His throat ached and his eyes burned. "Jake was like the father I never had. Such a good man. He hired me and trusted me when the only job I'd had since the navy was as a handyman at the mission. And later he sank thousands into the Tabernacle with no guarantee of repayment."

Holly let go of him and sat back, sensing his need to talk out his grief. "Did you tell him how you felt about him?"

"Yeah," Jim smiled sadly. "He tried to smack me, but I told him anyway. How do I not grieve, Holly? I'm glad he's happy with the Lord, but I wish he could have stayed a little longer."

"Where is it written that you shouldn't grieve? You lost a man you saw as a father figure. You miss him. He's left a hole in your life. I don't think God will think less of you for missing a good friend."

"No, but his wife and son and grandchildren look

to me for support. I can't fall apart every time his name comes up."

Holly cocked her head and smiled. "So today you look to me for support and we'll call it even for that little talking to you gave Ian. Okay?"

"Yeah. Okay. So do you think the kid will ever talk to me again?"

"Who? Ian? He's probably in his room thinking you don't want him for a son anymore. Why don't you go chat him up while I call the airline and confirm my flight."

"What's wrong?" Jim asked Ian when the boy looked from his plate, to him, and then back at his dinner again.

"What is this, Dad? Some sort of American dish?"

Couldn't he tell? "It's gravy bread."

"You put gravy on bread and that's supper?"

"Don't forget the green beans."

Ian eyed the vegetable suspiciously. "Why are they gray?"

"Look, I'm not the best cook, but this is one of my specialties. Try it. It's what all the kings and queens in Europe eat."

Ian rolled his eyes. "Uh, Dad. I've lived in Europe. That may work on a kid like Gracie but I know canned gravy when I see it. Don't worry, it'll be fine. I was just a bit surprised."

Jim dug in to his own triple-decker plate of gravy bread. It wasn't bad. The green beans were a little overcooked but at least he hadn't gotten caught up in his notes for tonight's Bible study and burned them the way he usually did. But Ian was a trooper. And they were having a good time in spite of his rather dubious culinary skills.

"Dad, what time do tonight's services start?"

"Half past seven. There's child care but the kids your age and up usually come into the service. You've been up since five, though, so if you want to sack out on the couch in my office, go ahead. Mrs. White will be in the office tonight. She can watch out for you."

"You've been up as long as I have and I wasn't working hard the way you were on that building. Is that going to be your house? Like a parsonage? Our pastor in London lived next to the church in a real house."

That had been Jim's original plan but the church had outgrown the barn so quickly that he'd abandoned plans for a little home of his own.

Besides which, he'd either need more space than it would provide for him, Holly and Ian, or he wouldn't need more than he had. It all depended on Holly. Which once again brought to his mind the worry that had been eating at him on and off since Monday. What besides his love—love that had failed her before—did he have to offer Holly? She was an accomplished woman used to dealing in international trade and treaties, and he pastored a church. And lived in two rooms without kitchen facilities.

"Dad!" Ian yelled.

Jim started. "Huh! Oh, Ian. Did I miss something?"

"You were staring at me, looking terribly sad."

Jim forced a smile. "Sad? Me? How could I be sad when I have you staying with me?"

"Well, you were, at least, quite far away. It's seven-ten. Didn't you say you needed to unlock the doors soon?"

Jim stood, his dinner forgotten. "Yeah, I'll go do that now. I usually stand by the door to the sanctuary and say hi to everyone as they arrive. Want to hang out there with me tonight?"

Ian's eyes brightened, lightening Jim's mood. "Sure thing!"

Ian peered around the corner up the hall toward his dad's office. It looked like the coast was clear. The last Sunday service was over and most everyone had gone home. Now all he had to do was get to the office where the Kids' Club had a meeting scheduled and he'd be home free. Free from ladies mussing his hair, and ladies pinching his cheeks, and ladies talking to him in squeaky voices they used on the babies in the nursery.

All week he'd been dragged from house to house while his dad helped the single ladies from the church with problems at their houses. Then they'd always asked him to dinner. At first, Ian had thought it was a good thing considering his father's cooking skills, but then he'd overheard one such lady talking to her mother. This was serious. Now he understood what they all wanted, and it wasn't their faucets fixed.

They wanted to marry his dad!

Ian sprinted into the office and slammed the door behind him breathing heavily.

"Good grief, boy, what's gotten in to you?" Mrs. White asked.

"Elise Mays. She almost caught up to me, but I gave her the slip."

Mrs. White nodded. "Ah. Her. I see your problem."

Ian gasped when someone tapped on the door behind him.

"Quick. Under here," Mrs. White motioned to the space under her desk. Ian scurried under just in time. "Oh, hello, dear. What can I do for you, *Mary Margaret?*"

"Have you seen dear little Ian?"

Oh, no! Not *Mary Margaret* Mays! She was worse than her sister Elise! Ian tried to shrink even farther under the desk.

"You're looking for Ian? Actually he's resting just now. Curled up like a little angel. He's a bit tired from all his running around. Pastor Jim doesn't want him to wear himself out. He has an appointment with his new doctor in the morning."

"Oh. Well, I suppose I should head on home. I thought I'd whip up a bit of dinner for our little dear and his father. I wanted to ask what he prefers. Well, I'll just take a chance then drop by with it later. Maybe we could have a picnic supper."

"I believe they have dinner plans already. And for tomorrow night, as well. I'll see you another time, dear." A few seconds went by. "You're safe now. The others are in your father's office waiting to start the meeting."

Ian climbed out. "Mrs. White, why doesn't my dad see that these ladies are after him?" he asked as he followed her into the inner office where Mickey, Daniel and Rachel sat on his father's leather sofa.

"Because he has eyes only for your mother. Which is good for us. Pastor Jim told me Holly is coming into the church to try untangling the books when she returns."

"But she's taking so long. Dad and I saw her on the telly Friday night as her meetings ended at the UN building. That's why I asked all of you to come for an emergency meeting. Ever since then Dad's been gloomy. He's fine for a while, then he just sort of stares off. He did it a few times before that but he's been terribly distracted ever since. And then there's all the ladies feeding us and pinching my cheeks. I've about had it!"

"I can see you have," Mrs. White said. "And I have an idea. We can try it when your mother gets back if we're all agreed."

Jim paced off the space again. He put his hands on his hips and shook his head. There was just no way that he could get more than a living room and a kitchen out of the first floor of the new building. The second floor he'd considered roughing in as storage space wasn't going to be high enough for more than one room in the middle and storage space around the perimeter.

"So, I'm back to square one, Lord," he muttered. He had nothing to offer Holly but his love in exchange for a successful, secure career. He had no idea how she felt about being the wife of a pastor, but she had to care whether she and Ian had a decent, comfortable place to live. There was no way his living quarters filled any of the usual requirements of a home except they were clean and in good repair.

How could he ask Holly to give up her apartment in New York and her successful career with the New Zealand government to marry him when he didn't even have a home to offer her? And on the salary he drew he didn't see himself affording one in the area anytime soon. Any apartment near enough to the church would cost almost as much per month as a house, so that was no solution. He couldn't even move into Trent's carriage house apartment with Holly and Ian because zoning restrictions didn't allow it to be rented to more than one adult and one child.

Shaking his head, he walked away from the new cement pad and back into the main building. He heard giggles coming from his office. "Hey, you guys. What's up?" he asked peeking around the doorway at the three oldest Osborne kids and Ian. Were Mrs. White not at the center of the huddle, he would have worried, but the older woman wouldn't let these four get away with any shenanigans.

"Oh, we were just hatching a secret plot," Mrs. White said airily.

Jim grinned. Mrs. White was such a character. "And what kind of plot would that be?"

The kids looked worried but a mysterious smile bloomed on Mrs. White's lined face. "Now if we shared it, it wouldn't be a very secret plot, would it?"

Chapter Twelve

Holly opened the door to the Tabernacle and peered inside, surprised to see rays of sunlight painting the flagstone floor of the foyer with color. After walking a few steps inside, she turned around to look up. Above the foyer that lay between the sanctuary, the offices and church kitchen, the walls vaulted to the roof angled to expose the full roof. Beams of amber and blue bounced and danced around the rough hewn timber high above.

The sunlight poured in through a mullioned window set in the opening left by the old hayloft's access door. A bronze-colored cross had been formed with the center lights of the window while the rest of the glass panes were tinted subtle tones of blue. With the exception of the hand-carved sign out on the highway and the necessary parking lot, the window was the only exterior sign that the 150-year-old barn was a church.

"It looks its best at this time of the day."

Holly's heart skipped a beat. Jim. She stared up at the cross. *Please let these feelings be coming from You, Lord. Don't let the decision I've made be of my own desire but Yours,* she prayed quickly. Then she closed her eyes and took a deep breath before pasting a smile on her face.

She turned. "I was surprised by the way it sparkles in the sunlight."

Jim stared at her for a few seconds then seemed to shake himself loose from some sort of trance. "That's…uh…" He cleared his throat and swallowed with what looked like great effort. "That's because there are a lot of imperfections in the glass. It's made of old salvaged glass that I found in a dump on the property." He stared at her for a few more tense seconds. "So have you come to bail me out?" he asked, then winced. "Sorry, bad connotation considering my—"

"Jim! Stop. You don't have to watch every word you say around me for fear it will let a bogeyman out of the closet. Yes, I've come to figure out what's gone wrong with the church's books. I'm hoping if I talk to Mrs. White she'll be able—" She stopped when she saw him grimace and shake his head. "What is it?"

"She's not coming in and won't be for at least two weeks. She told me on Sunday that her son and his family wanted her to go with them for a couple weeks at the shore. She hadn't been going but then she caved in and went along with them. Now not only are the books a mess, but the office is total chaos. The phone hasn't stopped all day.''

"So we're on our own with the accounting muddle.''

"And the ringing phone. Afraid so. Are you still game to try?" he asked.

"I don't believe I've ever met a column of numbers I didn't make friends with.''

Famous last words, Holly thought an hour later. The office phone rang incessantly and Jim seemed never to be able to slow down for even a moment to answer her questions. He had appointments all morning with people in need of his counsel and a long list of calls to return.

And Mrs. White wasn't the only one who had a problem with figures. Jim's system of reporting expenditures was to toss receipts in a shoe box. He drew no formal salary. What cash he needed, he took from petty cash or he used the church ATM and credit cards to make purchases. And he did little of either for himself. His entire life, until Ian had found him on the Internet, seemed to have been the Tabernacle or taking on home repair jobs to earn the money for his search for Ian.

By lunch she'd figured out one of the problems with the bookkeeping. Mrs. White somehow must have stumbled into the search-and-replace section of the program. She'd accidentally changed numbers at random throughout the spreadsheet for the entire fiscal year. Unfortunately, Holly couldn't tell how many or which ones she'd changed because there was no pattern.

After finding backup disks, she decided that the safest way to fix things would be to go back to the last good backup that Jake had done and then dig up and key in all deposits and expenses since. Jake Testa had been on holiday for a month and hadn't yet tackled the books after his return when he'd suffered his fatal attack. That left her six weeks worth of shoe box bookkeeping to unravel, as well. Holly was thankful that Mrs. White hadn't gotten past scrambling numbers.

"Hungry?" Jim asked her after he showed the last of his morning appointments to the door of his office.

Holly could picture the lunch she'd packed sitting on the kitchen counter at the apartment. It was a small wonder she hadn't forgotten her head considering how nervous she'd been that morning. "I forgot my lunch. I don't suppose takeout is very practical out here."

"This isn't the back beyond. We're very near every benefit of civilization here. But as luck would have it, someone dropped off a casserole for me last night. I guess she thought Ian was still here. I was in a peanut butter and jelly mood so it's still in the fridge and just needs heating."

Holly was appalled. "You ate peanut butter and jelly for dinner?"

Jim's grin was sheepish. "I thought it was better than ruining a perfectly good meal by trying to reheat it. My culinary ego took quite a beating last week courtesy of our son.''

"Your culinary ego?''

"Come on, don't try to pretend Ian didn't rat me out.''

"Rat you out?'' she asked with feigned confusion as she stood and leaned back against the desk. Ian, in fact, had been rather graphic about pancakes Jim had managed to somehow burn on the outside while leaving them still raw on the inside.

"I'm a terrible cook. You know it. I know it. It was easy to entertain Ian for the first few days. All I had to do was cook something and I had him rolling in the aisle.''

Holly laughed. "Oh, I wasn't pretending not to have heard. I was questioning that you could possibly *have* a culinary ego of any kind. Truthfully, I don't know which story I liked best. The hockey puck pork chops or the pasta-and-cheese soup. How have you survived this long?''

Jim shrugged. "I'm not terribly fussy about what I eat and I get a lot of dinner invitations from families in the church.''

"A good thing you aren't fussy,'' she muttered trying unsuccessfully to keep the amusement out of her voice.

"I was *trying* to give him healthy balanced meals.''

Oh, he was fun to tease! "As opposed to peanut butter and jelly. So you trimmed all the nasty fat off the pork chops and broiled them.''

"How was I suppose to know they'd shrink like

that? It was a shock when I pulled open the broiler and they were half the size they'd been.'' He grinned. ''But as Ian pointed out, at least that way there wasn't as much to choke down.''

''And the pasta soup?'' she asked, giving up on fighting a grin when she saw a blush rise to his cheeks in spite of his deep tan. This *had* been her favorite.

''The soup started life as a box of macaroni and cheese. Okay?'' Jim crossed his arms and leaned against the doorjamb. ''I misread the amount of milk. I was in a hurry for Sunday evening services and I thought the directions said two or three cups of milk. What they really said was two-thirds of a cup.''

''I hate to burst your bubble, Dad, but Ian didn't fall for the soup explanation. And did you really think a child as world traveled as Ian would believe all that kings and queens of Europe nonsense? Gravy bread for dinner? Queen Elizabeth isn't *that* frugal.''

''Hey, it worked on Grace and Daniel when I baby-sat once.''

Holly's laughter erupted drawing Jim's, as well. ''How about I reheat the casserole,'' she suggested out of kindness and self-defense.

''What a great idea! I'll be back in about ten or fifteen minutes. I have to meet the inspector out at the building site. Or did you want my help in the kitchen?'' His grin said he already knew the answer to that one.

Through the week as Holly input all recently filed transactions into the accounting software, she realized why Jim rarely had grocery bills to deduct. She noted that he ate abysmal meals—those he cooked for himself. On the whole, dinner invitations from church families did arrive as constantly as he'd said. Now she understood why all the women at the parties over the Independence Day weekend worried about how he ate. Someone had to.

He turned down most invitations because he said he suddenly had more food at the church than he knew what to do with. In fact, the influx of "leftovers," which were clearly not left over at all, clearly had him stumped.

She'd accepted one from a young woman earlier and had handed it to him a few minutes ago. "Another?" he'd said. "I guess we should have it for lunch. It's still warm. Think you could heat it up a little more? The inspector's here again to check on the water and sewer lines I ran this week. He's over there now." Jim frowned and looked at the casserole once more. "Who brought this again?"

"Her name and phone number are on the note on top," Holly told him smothering a laugh. Sometimes he reminded her of an absentminded professor.

"I don't recognize the name. Is she a new church member, did she say?"

Holly bit her lip. "No. She just asked that I give it to you. Maybe she heard about the undernourished local pastor and wanted to help."

Jim chuckled and scratched his head. "Well, I guess it's safe. I mean if it kills us, they'll know who did the deed. Right?" He set it on the desk then leaned down and kissed her on the cheek. "See you in ten."

Holly stared after him. He was a sweet man. Gentle. Caring. Often funny. And unfortunately for her heart rate a little too virile in his black T-shirt and jeans. So why had she not yet told him that she'd decided to give him the chance he'd asked for? What was holding her back? She thought maybe he knew, but she should say the words just the same.

She had just put the casserole in the oven and set the temperature when she heard a woman's voice calling for Jim. Not Pastor. Just Jim. That meant they were friends. Holly poked her head out into the hall. "May I help you?" she asked.

The woman was burdened with two full shopping bags. "Oh, hello. I just dropped by to see Jim. Where is he?"

Holly didn't like the woman's attitude. She seemed to think she was owed the information. "He's out at the building site. May I help you?"

"No. I'll just go talk to him."

"You shouldn't do that. He's with the building inspector and he's been terribly busy."

The woman smiled beatifically while still managing to look down her nose at Holly. "Oh, he won't mind. I just stopped by to take him on a picnic. Now that his son has gone, he'll have more time for fun with me."

Holly just gaped. A picnic. She was taking Jim on a picnic. She wanted to have *fun* with him. What did she mean *fun?* Who was this woman to assume Jim had no plans? And how long had she been in his life, anyway?

At the sound of the woman pelting down the hall, her shopping bags rattling and crackling, Holly pulled herself out of her musing. And stared in horrified wonder at the object of the first jealousy she'd ever felt.

Oh, this was too much! She was jealous of this woman and her ex-husband and she wasn't even certain she wanted him back. The very idea was ridiculous. But then she realized it wasn't ridiculous at all. She had been amused by all the meals when she'd looked up the names on the meals in the church directory and found most were members of the singles' Bible study. The young women clearly had a collective crush on their pastor.

But that Jim might be interested was something she'd never even considered. He seemed totally oblivious to the attention he garnered from women. And she understood completely why they were all so attentive.

To call Jim Dillon attractive was to say Gregory Peck had been passably nice-looking in his prime. The man was Hollywood handsome and unattached if you weren't bothered by his divorced status. Many Christians believed if a divorce took place before you found God, then there was no impediment to a future marriage. She had no idea how Jim felt about that, but the woman in pursuit of him right then certainly thought of him as available.

Holly frowned, remembering how sensitive Jim

was to anything that brought up their rocky past. How often could a man feel guilt and inferiority to a woman before she no longer interested him? How long before one of the bevy of cooking beauties zipping in and out of the church caught his eye? How long would he remain oblivious if she didn't at least tell him she was trying to move beyond yesterday and toward a future for them?

Holly paced across the kitchen to the stove and then back out into the hall. She turned around and gazed at the oven. Who cared who made the food? The man had to eat. What was her problem?

Honest as always with herself, Holly admitted the problem. She *was* jealous and it was an emotion she'd always thought rather unattractive. But did she have a right to feel envious?

Maybe she did. Jim had expressed an interest in her, hadn't he? He had asked for a chance to show her she could trust him and she was giving it to him. He had just casually kissed her cheek on his way out. So what right had he to stand her up to eat with Miss Picnic of Chester County?

Well, she wouldn't stand for it. And she certainly wouldn't eat some other woman's casserole. Before it got too warm, she'd just take it out and find one of the order-out delis Jim claimed were near! Better yet, she'd find one and go eat there!

"Oh, good, you took it out," Jim said. "Elise Mays packed us a picnic lunch. I'd hate to waste the opportunity to eat it fresh."

Holly thought her head would explode. "Don't

worry. You don't have to waste the opportunity. I'll go eat somewhere. I need a change of scenery.''

''But what about our picnic? Don't you want to eat outside? Is that it? I forget how unused you are to this kind of heat.''

Holly tossed the pot holder onto the counter. ''I'm perfectly fine with the heat. I've been in this country for two years,'' she said through gritted teeth then pivoted slowly to face him. He'd put the shopping bags on the counter. She looked around. ''Where's the bag lady?''

Jim chuckled. ''Well, that's one for the books. I never thought I'd hear anyone call Elise Mays a bag lady. She and her sister are in line to inherit about six million dollars apiece.''

''Oh, dear. Did I say that? I meant the lady with the bags.''

''She's on her way home. Why?''

Holly considered her ex-husband. Had he always been this oblivious to female advances? No, he certainly had not. All she'd done the night they met was smile at him and he'd gotten the message that she was interested. ''Ms. Mays expected to eat it with you. You have to know that. She's much less subtle than all the others.''

''Others? You mean her sister?''

''I mean your singles' Bible-study-turned-cooking club.''

''I haven't any idea why they've suddenly gone into cooking overdrive.''

Holly grinned. He was embarrassed. She walked

around the counter and looked up at him. "The singles are doing the same thing as Ms. Mays. They're trying to attract your attention. The way to a man's heart and all that." She poked his stomach.

Jim snatched her hand and clutched it gently against his chest. "I don't think so. Elise and her sister Mary Margaret aren't members here but everyone else knows what woman I want in my life."

"And who might that woman be?"

He pushed her hair back and cupped her cheek, his eyes vital and fervent. Then he bent his head as if to kiss her. "She's someone I probably don't deserve. You," he whispered against her lips. "Only ever you." This kiss like that last one on the Fourth of July grabbed Holly by the heart and squeezed. Jim was the only man whose kisses had ever been able to steal her breath and her sanity in a millisecond.

Holly reached up to wrap her arms around his neck, but he pulled back and turned half away, leaning the heels of his hands on the edge of the tall counter. "This is a *bad* idea," he said with a quaver in his voice.

"You sound afraid. Of me?" She noted her voice wasn't all that steady, either.

He looked at her, the expression in his hazel eyes, intense and grave. "Afraid? Me? Holly, I'm terrified of you and what I feel for you. How's that for telling the truth? Please, let's get out of here. We'll have our picnic. Outside where anybody who drives up can see us." He checked the bags. His hands were unsteady.

"In fact, there's enough food here for an army. Shall we go pick up Ian?"

Holly nodded, as shaken by their kiss and the desire that had sparked between them as Jim was. Maybe they should make sure they weren't alone. She'd bring Ian with her while she was helping fill in for Mrs. White to act as a buffer—a chaperon. But how much fun would that be for an eight-year-old? She'd have to bring Mickey or Rachel or even odd little Daniel to keep him company.

Holly's gaze locked with Jim's. The lighter specks in his eyes seemed to glitter. Maybe they'd better bring all three.

Chapter Thirteen

Jim swung around in his chair, distracted from his work on Sunday's sermon by Holly's laughter in the outer office. He looked at the glass wall between the two offices and opened the blinds enough to just glance at her. But, as always, a glance at Holly wasn't enough. She sat at the desk with Daniel standing next to her. She kissed the boy on the cheek and he—tough guy Daniel—hugged her in return. Jim chuckled quietly. For a week and a half she'd enchanted every kid who'd come through the door.

He'd had no idea how absolutely wonderful she was with children. Children of all ages swarmed to her seeking one of her magical smiles. She'd even taken the time to learn how to sign a few words to Kara Kelly, the deaf daughter of the woman who helped out with the cleaning. And when she arrived every day with the kids, she had plans that made their days at the church special.

Jim twisted back to his desk but couldn't seem to concentrate on work. He put his head back and closed his eyes, reliving the precious moments during the picnic when Holly had given him hope for a future together.

A cold front had begun to move in, cooling the day by the time they got back to the church with the kids in tow. Thunderstorms were forecast because of the front. For their picnic they'd settled close to shelter in the shadow of the church.

Once lunch was eaten, the children had raced off for the swing set. That put them within sight to help keep the intimacy of the situation in hand, but he and Holly were alone enough to talk privately. And they had certainly talked…

Jim had stretched his legs out in front of him into the space left by the kids. He propped himself up on his elbows and dropped his head back to watch the clouds scud across the sky as the breeze ruffled the surrounding trees.

"This was quite nice," Holly said and started packing up the leftover fried chicken. "Ms. Mays is a rather good cook."

"Now who's naive?" he said with a chuckle. "The family cook probably whipped this up. Elise would probably need a map to find their kitchen. Not only is she hopelessly spoiled, would you believe she's twenty-one? Her sister, who's nearly a carbon copy, is not quite twenty."

"Oh, that can't be!"

"We've been out here for five years. They were

neighbors of Jake's. Jake and his wife brought the whole family out here the day we tore the old roof off. They were sixteen and fifteen. They were *advanced* even then. They've been popping in now and again ever since. They are the reason for the glass wall in my office. Mrs. White suggested it to protect my reputation, but she usually protects me from them altogether.''

Holly snickered. "But besides worry for your pastoral reputation, I bet it gives you the willies to be looked at like a sex object. Doesn't it?"

Jim turned his head and stared at Holly. How could she be so perceptive about some things and still not see that he'd truly changed? He nearly said as much but settled for a less confrontational observation. "You never saw through me that easily when we were married."

Holly's green eyes grew suddenly serious. "Shall we be honest? I not only didn't see through you, I'm afraid I never saw you at all. I saw what I wanted to see. Cinderella and her Prince Charming."

Jim looked away again at the darkening sky. "Except when you kissed the prince, he turned into a frog."

Holly put her hand over his. "As you once pointed out, I decided who you were and then hated you when I turned out to be wrong."

"I was angry that morning," Jim said soberly. "You'd just made all my worst fears come true. I lashed out unfairly at you, hoping to hurt you as much as I thought you were hurting me. I know the truth. So don't you doubt that girl's wisdom.''

"I don't know about wise as much as foolish. I hope I've grown as a person since then. I find myself disliking that shallow girl who still believed in fairy tales.''

Jim turned his hand over and enfolded hers as he twisted to his side to face her. With his free hand he pushed her hair back behind her ear so he could see her precious face better. ''Don't. She wasn't shallow or foolish. She was just in way over her head with a character like me. But I loved her, Holly. I still do.''

"Jim, I still don't know if I can forget the pain and betrayal that girl felt back then. But I'm trying to look past the yesterdays and see the present clearly. And I've put the future in God's hands. I hope that's enough for now.''

"That's where I've been putting my future for years. It isn't a bad place,'' he told her. Her announcement was more than he'd hoped for a few short weeks earlier, but now it wasn't nearly enough. He hadn't let Holly know he felt pressured and desperate. He didn't want to rush her, but the six weeks for Ian's initial study seemed to be flying by. And then they'd be headed back to New York.

It had seemed like such a long time in the beginning. Then once she'd gotten there and he'd realized how hard letting her go would be, he'd set out to prove himself, still thinking he had plenty of time. But six weeks had turned out to be only five when she'd left for New York. He had only two weeks left to win her trust and her heart or he'd have to do it long distance.

And now he'd realized that even if she did learn to trust him, he still had a major problem to work out before he could ask her to stay and marry him again. He couldn't believe how shortsighted he'd been. How could he not have thought ahead to where they'd live if he did win Holly's heart again?

Nor had he considered how Holly felt about being the wife of a pastor. Some women couldn't take sharing their men with a whole congregation. It was often a discussion among fellow pastors at conferences and seminars. And Holly already knew it wasn't a particularly easy role because of her parents' difficulties. She might not feel too kindly toward the idea.

Of course, it wouldn't be as if she'd be forced to run women's clubs and such as had been expected of her mother. The Tabernacle wasn't a social club the way her father's parish had been. She wouldn't be forced into doing anything she didn't feel led to do by the Lord. But still, she might not know that. And he hadn't a clue how to tell her without sounding presumptuous. He couldn't ask how she felt about his housing worries, either. She'd probably think it was too soon and that he was rushing her as he had nine years ago.

Holly's laughter blended with Daniel's again and Jim fought off his depressing thoughts. Maybe it was time to find out what was so funny and to quit being so negative. If a reconciliation between them was to be, the Lord would find a way. He quietly opened the door but neither Daniel nor Holly seemed to notice. They were too busy with their heads bent over a book.

"Now look here, Daniel. Here are some old expressions that come from Jesus Himself. Let's write these down and we'll look them up later. 'The blind leading the blind.' Luke 6:39. 'Cast your pearls before swine.' Matthew 7:6. Oh, and here's the one you asked me about. 'Don't let your right hand know what the left is doing.' Matthew 6:3."

"Well, it sure sounds like you're right. Jesus did start a lot of this stuff," Daniel conceded.

Jim stepped back and listened while Holly found all the verses and explained the context in which Jesus had spoken and how His words had filtered into the language as popular clichés. Then she sent Daniel off to play with the others.

"Now there's an interesting way to spark a Bible study."

Holly twirled around in her chair and beamed a smile straight to Jim's heart. "You heard. He's so intelligent. And hungry for any knowledge. He's actually a delight. I thought if I channeled his incessant questions into researching the clichés instead of just asking about them it might make life easier for everyone."

"Or harder. You never know with Daniel."

Holly chuckled sending fingers of tension along his spine. "You never know with most children. I think it's the nature of the beast."

"This is going to sound stupid considering how great Ian has turned out but I hadn't realized what a gift you have with children. You always seem to know exactly what each of them needs."

"I practically raised Alan and Christie, so I'd had a lot of practice when Ian came along." Her accompanying shrug was a little too careless for his liking.

"No. It's more than that. You have a real gift. Having experience with them isn't all it is. I've had parents working in Sunday school classes who can't seem to relate to other people's kids."

Holly's blush reminded him of something he'd already known but had forgotten. She'd had very little praise in her life. "I can't tell you how much I've appreciated your helping out this way. I'll be sorry to see Mrs. White come back. She's a big help, but I'm going to miss hearing your voice and turning around and seeing you here like this. New York's so far away."

Holly looked away making Jim wonder if he'd overstepped yet again.

"Are you coming to Trent and Maggie's for dinner?" she asked. "I heard something about sirloin steak on the grill."

"Wouldn't miss it. We've discussed why I never turn down a meal," he quipped. "Well, I guess it's back to work."

Now that wasn't very honest, he chided himself as he closed the door and the blinds between the offices. But it had been much more prudent than admitting that he never gave up an opportunity to be with her, either. That would have been almost as dumb as mentioning her return to New York in that hangdog way.

He looked down at his notes, but, some minutes later, he shut his notebook. This wasn't going anywhere. All he could think of was Holly. He decided to reverse his usual schedule and head out to the building project for a little manual labor before he said something else stupid to Holly. He'd work on the sermon later.

"This meeting of the Kids' Club will now come to order. Ian, what has you worried?" Mickey wanted to know.

"Operation Wedding Ring isn't moving fast enough. We leave in two weeks. We have to *do* something! Mom keeps making us come here with her. It's like she doesn't want to be alone with Dad."

"And poor Mrs. White went away with her bossy son just so Pastor Jim would need help in the office. What went wrong? They sure looked at each other all moony that day after Mrs. Dillon fixed the figures we messed up," Rachel said. "Ian's right. We have to think of something."

"Today it's worse than it has been. Dad always waits to go outside to work till Mom leaves. Today he's out there already and it isn't even lunchtime."

"There has to be a way to get them together and keep them together for a while where one or the other of them can't go running off to do something," Mickey said.

"Remember when Mrs. White locked herself in the supply closet? We could lock them in there for a while," Daniel suggested.

"No. Mum doesn't like close spaces."

"Ian, that makes it perfect," Rachel assured him.

"It's perfect to terrify my mum? I don't think so."

"Boys. You never think past the obvious. He'd have to help her stay calm. And then he'd have to rescue her and be her hero."

"So how do we get them both in there?" Daniel asked.

"Wait! I'm still not so sure," Ian protested.

"Do you have a better idea?" Mickey asked.

Ian shook his head in defeat.

It did sound as if it could work as long as Dad was there to keep her calm.

Mickey got his great-idea look all of a sudden. "I've got it. That's where the circuit breakers are. We go throw a bunch of them especially the ones for the closet, office and foyer. Daniel hates the dark so he can stay in the classroom where there are still lights and windows. He's our excuse."

"What kind of excuse?" Daniel asked suspiciously.

"You'll see. Rachel goes to get Pastor Jim. Ian, you talk your mom into trying to fix them, but we make sure Pastor Jim is just about at the church with Rachel when you take her to the closet. Timing will be everything. I'll be the lookout and run down and tell you when. Okay, Rachel and Ian? Think you can handle your assignments?"

Ian thought perhaps Mickey was a bit carried away with the spy novel he was reading and he felt a bit funny about this.

"My dad tells me never to lie. This feels like lying."

"And I still don't know why I'm an excuse," Daniel added.

"First. We won't lie. You say to your mom, 'Daniel's afraid of the dark. Could you fix the lights? Mickey told me where the electrical box is. He's with Daniel.' And I *will* be. I'll be with him watching Rachel run across the field with Pastor Jim."

Ian felt remarkably better. "I suppose then I wouldn't be lying at all. This is grand. Shall we get started?"

"We should synchronize our watches," Mickey suggested.

"Daniel and I don't have watches," Ian pointed out.

"Oh. Too bad. We'll just have to wing it."

"Wing it?" Daniel asked.

Mickey and Rachel both rolled their eyes. Daniel made them do that a lot. "You can look it up later, Daniel," Mickey said and clapped his hands like the platoon leader in the movie they'd watched this morning. "Let's move, troops. Operation Blackout starts now!"

Holly looked around Jim's office. Where on earth was he? He'd disappeared into his office around ten, just after she and Daniel finished with the cliché book. He'd seemed rather upset when he'd gone back in. She hoped it hadn't been because of her. But she hadn't been able to help her reaction to the idea of returning to her life in New York.

She hadn't felt quite comfortable on arrival there last week. The noise and the traffic had frazzled her nerves on her way to work from the airport and later that night it had kept her awake. By the next morning she'd realized she missed Jim every bit as much as she did Ian. Right then she'd been tempted to ask the ambassador's help in changing her status with immigration and in finding a job in the Philadelphia area.

She'd been tempted but something had held her back. It still did. She knew Jim had changed. And she knew that if he ever started drinking again, it wouldn't be because he didn't love her or the Lord. But innumerable people had tried and failed to keep him on the narrow path of sobriety. Her mother had stopped drinking for eight years during which time she'd given birth to Alan and Christie.

But something had set her off again and nothing had ever been the same. Holly didn't know what she would do if she went back to Jim and he turned from God to a bottle again as her mother had. The damage to Ian and to her would be crushing.

Holly clenched her hand and the message she'd taken for Jim crinkled in her fist. In the next instant the lights went out and the air-conditioning shut off. Holly froze in the doorway between the offices. It was surprisingly dark, with only a modicum of light filtering in through the hall and loft window over the foyer. Her claustrophobia suddenly reared its ugly head, making breathing a bit difficult. While she talked herself into believing that the room was the same size it had been with the lights, she saw a beam of light arc across the room. "Mum? Are you in here?"

"Oh, Ian, you have a torch. Wonderful."

"It's called a flashlight here, Mum."

Holly chuckled. Ian just loved learning and using new American names for common things. "I wonder if this is a widespread blackout," she thought aloud.

"I don't think so," Ian said. "Other parts of the building are on. Could you throw the circuit breakers back on, do you think? Daniel's afraid of the dark. Mickey told me where they are. He's...uh, he's watching Daniel. This way. Come on, Mum."

Holly moved toward Ian. "All right. Lead the way." It was always much better to do something than stand around feeling out of control and helpless. "But if it's too complicated, we'll have to go find your father."

Following Ian and his beam of light made Holly feel more in control and less antsy. Ian stopped at a door near the back of the building. "Here it is. Mickey said the box is on the back wall."

Holly looked at the cavernous closet. At least it wasn't too small. "Give me the light, poppet." She took the torch. Now that she was in control of the light, she felt even better. "Well, in for a penny in for a pound," she quipped then went in. It didn't take long to locate the big gray electrical box.

"I'll get it," Jim said from behind her just as she

opened the box. He was suddenly next to her. "Sorry I wasn't here. Thanks, Rach—" He stopped in mid-sentence and moved back toward the door. She heard something then, an ominous "Uh-oh," from Jim.

"What's wrong?" she asked, panic rising in her.

"Holly, sweetheart. Do you still have that little problem with closed-in spaces?"

Holly stared in horror at the door—the closed door. The closed door with the doorknob Jim was shaking.

"Tell me we aren't locked in here," she said, trying to keep the desperation out of her voice. "Please."

Jim turned and he gripped her shoulders gently. "Calm down. I'll get the lights on and you'll feel better. Then we'll just yell for the kids and they'll unlock the door."

Seconds later the light was on and he shouted for the children. Then he pounded and shouted some more. To no avail. All the while Holly looked on in fascinated horror. They were locked in.

"Where could they be?" she asked, not at all surprised by the quaver in her voice.

"Maybe they went outside to the play yard," Jim said and turned to her.

Holly guessed she must look pretty bad, because he wrapped her in his arms. Something he'd been studiously avoiding. Holly rested her head on his shoulder. "Please get us out of here."

"I will, honey. Just try to calm down. Talk to me."

"What about?"

"Tell me what you did this morning."

Holly forced herself mentally back at the desk in the nice big office she'd been occupying. "I finished the bulletin for Sunday. Took messages. Oh!" She remembered the message still clutched in her hand. "I took a message for you. It's from a man. Joshua Daniels. It was odd. His voice sounded a bit familiar but the name doesn't ring a bell."

"Not odd at all. Let's sit down and I'll tell you about it."

Jim pushed a couple boxes of paper into the middle of the room and sat on one. Holly moved quickly back into the comfort of his arms.

"This is quite a story," he said as he hugged her close. "Remember the painting over the fireplace?"

"The one painted by Cassidy Jamison Daniels. You said it was a gift for conducting her wedding ceremony to your navy friend."

"Well, David Chernak *is* Joshua Daniels."

"That was him? Then he not only changed his name he lost his accent, as well. I always knew it was David calling because of that Southern drawl."

"Actually, he lost more than his accent. He lost his memory as well. No one knows what happened to him but the speculation is that he was car jacked, beaten and left for dead. An older couple found him but he had no identification. He was in a coma for six months and the police had no luck finding his family."

"Why didn't Regina look for him?"

"Because he'd left her and his family's business to start a new life. He'd learned that Regina and his brother were having an affair and that his parents had known about it. He told them if he ever forgave any of them he'd contact them."

"How awful. He must have been devastated."

"We can only imagine because when he came out of the coma he'd lost his memory completely. Speech included. He's had to relearn everything, and with the help of the couple who found him, he's built a wonderful life, and is the pastor of a church in the mountains. I found him by accident and helped him fill in some of the blanks of his past."

"Which is why you didn't have a problem with his marrying again?" Holly shivered.

"Are you chilly?"

"A little. Yes. Now that you mention it." She looked up. "Why is there a vent in a closet?"

He chuckled. "Because believe it or not, this is really a small room that we use as a big closet. It was actually supposed to be a prayer room. But when the walls went up, I shifted the plans. It's ironic. I thought of you the first time I walked in here. It felt too small to be a room, so I put this wide shelving in here and turned it in to a nice big closet."

"It doesn't feel all that big. And why does a closet have a lock on the outside?"

Jim tightened his arms in comfort. "I switched the knob around when one of the kids whose parents I was counseling locked himself in here to have a temper tantrum. I meant to get a different kind of knob but it slipped my mind."

"Maybe we should shout for them again," she suggested.

Jim frowned and glanced up at the vent. "No. I have a feeling they aren't going to hear us. I have a better idea than screaming ourselves hoarse. But I'm going to have to let go of you. Will you be okay?"

Holly had gotten so comfortable nestled against his broad chest that she'd forgotten about the smallness of the room. She looked up into his eyes and nodded. She didn't want him to ever let go of her and the light in his eyes said the same. "I don't think I'll fall apart unless you intend to crawl through that duct."

His smile said that was exactly his latest plan.

"Couldn't you just pick the lock?"

Jim chuckled. "I may look like Agent 007, but I don't have his talents."

Holly laughed softly. "So you know you look like him."

"I've heard it," he said, his disgust evident. "I just don't buy the dream. And no. I have no idea how to pick a lock. I said I grew up rough—not criminal." Jim kissed her forehead and let her go.

Bereft of his nearness, Holly shivered. "This closet really gets cold," she said, rubbing her arms.

She thought Jim muttered, "Not cold enough," as he shifted the heavy boxes of paper around, but the scuffling noise muffled his words. "There's a vent in the hall. I just have to get that far," he explained. He plucked a little square of metal out of a leather pouch on his belt. She watched in amazement while he transformed it into a pair of pointed pliers. "Then I'll unscrew the vent with these and let the vent drop out. I'll follow it, hopefully with a lot more grace than crashing to the floor like the vent. Then I'll unlock the door and you're out. Five minutes tops. You can hang in that long. Can't you, sweetheart?''

Holly swallowed, unable to guard her heart against the concern and gentleness in his eyes. ''As long as I don't have to follow you out through there,'' she said, pointing to the vent. She gulped this time. It looked so narrow. ''How will you fit through there? What if you get stuck?''

Jim smiled tenderly. ''Now don't go getting claustrophobic on my account. It'll be a tight fit but I think I can get through.'' He stood on the first box and unfolded the tool in several directions. Soon he'd transformed the little square tool into a screwdriver and climbed another of the steps he'd created. Not long after that he handed her the cover and the screws.

''Well, here I go.''

''I don't understand why Ian insisted I fix the circuit breakers if he knew you were on the way.''

Jim looked down at her, his eyes narrowed. ''Believe me when I say there *will* be an inquisition.''

Holly giggled and watched nervously as he boosted himself into the duct and started to shimmy forward. She couldn't resist following him up the box steps to see how much room he had in there. And she was sorry she did. How he was able to even exhale escaped her.

Dizzy suddenly, Holly sat on the top box and stared at the door willing it to open. Breathing became a chore, giving her a firsthand look at how Ian felt when his asthma flared up. Though it seemed to take an eternity before she heard Jim yell that he was on his way out of the duct, she knew by her watch that it wasn't very long at all. Then at last the door opened.

Holly launched herself into Jim's waiting arms. "Fix that. Please. What if it had been one of the children? They could have been scarred for life."

Jim let go of Holly. The *children* weren't out of the woods yet, he thought and gritted his teeth as he knelt to remove the latch-bolt assembly. Not by a long shot were they out of the woods, he stewed while disassembling the doorknob. It wasn't a permanent solution but it beat having four little practical jokers lock Holly in there again. "This won't be happening again," he said and stood.

Holly reached up and plucked a tuft of dust from his hair. "My hero. Thank you for being so sweet. I know I get irrational in tight places."

"And I'm sorry I didn't do something about that before now. If I had, we couldn't have been locked in."

"Well, it isn't as if they did it on purpose. Rachel and Ian mustn't have realized it was locked. And speaking of the children, I guess we should check on them."

He looked at her pale face and still shaking hands. Oh no, he wanted the pleasure of checking on them himself. Besides which, he didn't want her feelings hurt. And they would be if she found out that the children she'd been trying so hard to entertain had played so cruel a practical joke on her.

He scooped her up into his arms. "Right now I want you to lie down on the sofa in my office. You're still not too steady on your feet. I'll check on them. Believe me, I can't wait to check on them."

Minutes later Jim closed the door to his office and stalked down the hall. They weren't in his rooms, so he went hunting and found them on the playground. "Having a nice time all of you?" he asked.

They all looked—smug! "This is smashing equipment, Dad. Better than Peter Cooper has on their playground," Ian said with a cheeky grin as Holly would say.

Jim felt his blood pressure soar. With pretend calm, he leaned against a big upright post and crossed his arms. "I am just waiting with bated breath to hear why all of you thought locking us in that closet was funny."

"You ate worms?"

Jim shot Daniel a look that widened the boy's eyes in alarm. Daniel didn't pursue his question.

"I'm waiting," Jim reminded them when silence reigned. "And while you're all thinking, I'd like to know how you thought we'd get out of there with all of you out here having a high old time!"

"Oh, we'd have let you out in a while," Rachel said cheerfully.

Jim just stared at all four little monsters. He looked at his watch. "It's one o'clock. All four of you will go into the church and sit in separate pews in the sanctuary until we leave for dinner. And I'd like you to think about Holly lying on my sofa emotionally exhausted because she was so terrified. And one more thing just for the record. It wasn't funny. Not by a long shot.''

"We're sorry, Dad.''

"Yeah, Pastor Jim. Should we say we're sorry to Mrs. Dillon?'' Mickey asked.

"This is between you and me and maybe Trent and Maggie. But I don't want Holly's feelings hurt thinking you'd want to frighten her this way. She loves you all very much, and she thinks it was an accident. I think we'll keep it that way. Now march. Front pews. One of you in each one.''

Jim watched them scurry off. Anybody who thought being a parent was easy was nuts. Just plain nuts!

Chapter Fourteen

It was one of those difficulties of parenthood that had Jim going with Trent on his evening run. He knew he had to tell Trent what his kids had done. He just didn't know how to bring it up. But Trent had come to know him well. As soon as they were out of sight of the house, he slowed to a walk.

"So, what did my angels do today?"

"How did you know?"

"They all watched you through dinner like a flock of hawks, and I think Rachel paled six shades when you said you were coming with me. Always remember she's their weak link. Caves in every time." Jim laughed at Trent's siege mind-set then told him the story of the practical jokers and the locked closet.

"I can't believe they thought it was funny. Holly was terrified. They couldn't have upset her more if they'd set out to torture her."

"I think we can think of a little torture to put them through tomorrow. Kids. You can't live with them, you can't live without them." Trent sent him a piercing look. "Or is that women?" he asked pointedly.

The future suddenly weighed heavily on Jim's shoulders. "I'm trying to figure out how to avoid doing either."

"Oh? And here I thought you were trying for heatstroke, exhaustion or both? I couldn't help noticing a ridiculous amount of prep work already done on the new building. Work I thought the bunch of us were supposed to do together next weekend."

"There'll be plenty to do. And I don't work in the heat of the day. And if I weren't doing that, I'd sit around thinking and driving myself nuts. I still think and drive myself nuts but at least this way I'm accomplishing something and working off enough nervous energy so that I can sleep."

"Want to talk about it?"

Jim nodded. "Let me ask you something, if you were a woman—"

Trent's snicker cut him off. "Now there's a stretch."

Jim gave him a friendly shove. "I'm serious. I'll reword it for the less mature among us. What do I have to offer Holly? She has a highly visible, successful career. She has a terrific apartment in New York and she makes probably ten times what I do a year."

"That wouldn't be too hard to do. As far as I can see, what you draw can hardly be considered a salary and as the church grows you have less time for side jobs."

"Look, I'm not complaining about money."

"Of course you're not. If you have one fault it's that you undervalue yourself. You should be paid a set salary. One a lot higher than what the last financial reports show you drawing. The board's been remiss in not just handing you one."

"I can't put a dollar value on service to the Lord. I love what I do. I never expected to get rich at it."

"I'm not talking about getting rich nor am I asking you to come up with a figure. But your board can put a dollar value on all you do. We have to."

Jim felt terrible. "That isn't why I brought this up. I just needed to talk to someone. Besides, for some time to come, a set salary isn't going to solve the biggest problem I have. I don't have a home to offer Holly, and it will take way too long to save money for a down payment on a place around here. How can I ask her to live the way I do till then?"

Trent veered to the roadside. "Pull up a hunk of fence," he suggested as he climbed to the top rail.

Jim was too keyed up to sit still so he just leaned against the post. "Look, the way I live has suited me just fine. Please don't think I'm saying I've been dissatisfied but—"

"It still only has two rooms and a bath. No kitchen. And you eat on the fly or in the conference room. A little tough to have family dinners with no kitchen of your own."

"Exactly. If Holly and Ian wind up with me, I'm

going to need more room. The original plan was to use the framework of the new building but it's still too small for three people.''

Trent got a sudden gleam in his eye. "I don't think we should abandon the idea of a house on the property. What would you say to a rental property until the church can build a house? I'd have to talk it over with Maggie first, but I may have a solution if you're willing.''

"Anything's better than this merry-go-round in my head. I've tried to give it to the Lord and let Him handle it, but for the first time, He just seems to hand it right back to me.''

Trent grinned. "Maybe that's so you could talk to the one person who can solve your problem. Me. Or rather, Maggie. When we got back together, she had bought that little house on Surrey Lane. We've been renting it out but the renters moved out yesterday. I was over there this morning and they haven't taken good care of it. Frankly, the whole place, top to bottom, needs a major cleaning and painting. Maggie really needs me at home right now with the kids out of school and her feeling so terrible all the time, so I can't do the work any time soon. If Maggie agrees, and I see no reason she wouldn't, the house is yours to rent. You can do the work and I'll supply whatever you need for a reduction in rent. How's that sound?''

Jim was once again bowled over by the way the Lord worked in the lives of His people. He smiled. "It sounds as if I don't have as big a problem as I thought I did. Thanks, Trent. This is at least one worry off my mind. Now I only have to convince Holly to give marriage to me a second chance."

"Maybe you could take her over there after it's cleaned and let her help decide on colors and such."

"Yeah, maybe I'll do that. Let me know what Maggie says and I'll get on cleaning it."

Holly checked her hair in the mirror by the door again. Jim had called and asked her to go out with him sans Ian. A date, he'd said. He'd planned the whole day. They were going to a couple of museums and a Revolutionary battlefield. When she'd asked why he wanted to exclude Ian, he'd said there were things they needed to talk about and that Ian shouldn't be there when they did.

Now she wished she hadn't asked. She'd only been curious. And now she was afraid. What if he planned to ask her to marry him? What would she say? She didn't want to say no. But she was afraid to say yes.

A knock on the door startled her and her hairbrush flew out of her hand, bouncing off the screen right in front of Jim's face.

"Was it something I said?" he asked with a crooked smile.

The bass undertone in his voice seemed to play along her spine. "No, it was me being jumpy. Too much time on my hands these days, I guess. I miss working at the church. Is Mrs. White settling in all right?"

"Mrs. White isn't nearly as pretty as you no matter how much help she is." He opened the door and bent to retrieve the brush. "Your hair's perfect." He stepped behind her and she met his eyes in the mirror for a drawn-out moment. Then he grinned and stroked the brush through her hair. "Smells perfect, too. I've missed you these last couple days, Holly. I wish Mrs. White's son had decided to stay an extra week or so."

Holly smiled. She couldn't help it. She'd missed him, too. It was getting so she couldn't imagine her life without him in it. She reached to take the brush and drew a quick breath when their hands touched. "I came out for lunch yesterday," she reminded him and started fussing with her hair again. Not so much to make improvements but for something to do other than stare into his magnetic gaze through the mirror.

Jim shook his head and stepped aside to lean a shoulder against the wall next to the mirror. He took the brush back, avoiding any contact and set it on the table. "It wasn't nearly enough time. I got spoiled seeing you every day. Knowing you were near."

Holly's stomach flipped. They had to get out of there! "We have all day together. Let's not waste it. I'm ready and Ian's been handed over to Maggie and Trent since ten o'clock. Just let me get my purse. So, where are we going first?"

"It's a surprise. I hope a good one. It's not too far."

Ten minutes later on a road she recognized as close to the church, he pulled into a driveway. "What's this?" she asked.

"My new home. I'm going to be renting it until we can put up a house on the church property. That still may be a while because we have a policy of not taking out mortgages. I've always felt that if God wants us to do something, He'll provide the means. So far it's worked.

"I know the house doesn't look like much right now. The last renters beat it up a bit. But it's nothing paint, paper and a little landscaping won't cure. Come on. I wanted you to see it. Maybe give me some advice on colors and the like."

Holly stared after him as he jumped out of the truck to come around to get her door. He wanted her advice? From what she'd heard, he'd done every bit of the decision making on the church from working with the architect to the color palette. He hardly needed her advice. She was an import-export expert, not a decorator.

Jim opened her door and put his arm around her, leading her up the winding front walk. He let go to unlock the door, then stepped inside and held open the screen door for her. "It's pretty hot in here. Let me get the air-conditioning up and running," he said walking off to one side of the foyer into what looked like the dining room to adjust the thermostat.

"So this is going to be where you'll be living," she asked.

"After the work's done. The week Ian stayed with me showed me that my rooms at the church are kind of limited."

"I've only seen them, but Ian didn't complain. He loved having the run of the church."

Jim grinned, but she could see it was forced. "I

somehow doubt you'd enjoy sleeping on a sofa bed and cooking in the church kitchen."

Holly's stomach turned over. How had he meant that? "It isn't my place to judge your lifestyle except where it impacts Ian and as I said, he didn't mind."

His grin slipped. "I was kind of hoping and praying that you'd be willing to step into a place where it is your business."

Oh dear. Here comes the impossible question. "Jim, I don't think I'm—"

Jim gripped her shoulders. "Holly, wait. Please. I love you. You know that. I've done everything I can think of to convince you that the change in me is real and lasting. What else can I do? I live my life for the Lord. I cherish every second I spend with you. I need you, Holly, love."

"You promised not to pressure me." Looking at the desperation and love in his eyes hurt.

"I'm not trying to pressure you. Honestly. I can certainly live without you, but there'd be this empty spot in me and my life that only you will ever fill. I know your bringing Ian down here for treatment wasn't supposed to be about us, but that's what's happened. There are feelings between us. Strong ones. They've been there every time we've touched. The times we've kissed. You've felt them, too."

"I'm not denying that or that I care. It's just that this has all been very unsettling. I never expected to feel this way about anyone again, least of all you. But getting to know you the way you are now has been wonderful. You have changed. I just haven't decided what to do about it yet.''

He took her face in his hands. "Come back to me." He kissed her and her world spun crazily. "Come be my love. Come be my wife," he begged.

Holly reached up and cupped his cheek. "I need more time."

He let go of her and turned away, jamming his hands in his front pockets. She could tell by the rigid set of his jaw that he was angry. "How much time will be enough, Holly?" he wanted to know, as he pivoted back to face her again. "When we're fifty and I'm still not drinking, will you believe me then? And if you do believe me then, how are you going to feel about all the wasted years?" His lips were pursed, his eyes glittering with suppressed anger.

His anger didn't surprise her at all, but the sense his question made did. It was something she hadn't considered. How would she feel? She reached out and put her hand on his forearm. "A few more days. Bring me back here in a few more days and we'll decide if we're putting your furniture or mine in the parlor."

He blinked, clearly surprised by her change. "Sunday? We'll come back Sunday?"

Holly nodded. "Sunday. I'll give you my answer then."

"But you'll still come over for a movie with Ian after the crew leaves on Saturday?"

"We'll be there. And today after we do some exploring here, I still expect to see the museums and this Brandywine Battlefield you promised to take me to. I believe you mentioned that you rebels were trounced by King George's troops there.''

The anger was clearly gone from his eyes when he said, ''Of course we'll still go. Actually it's the perfect place for today.''

''Oh?''

He shrugged then smiled, clearly finding his good humor once more. ''Sure. We lost the battle but we won the war, didn't we?''

By Saturday morning, as Holly packed a picnic lunch for Ian and the four Osborne children in preparation for their day at Valley Forge Park, she still hadn't decided the outcome of her own personal war. She guessed going to yet another battlefield was an apropos way to spend the last day of her reprieve.

She felt as if her heart already stood on one side of the chasm called marriage, and her mind teetered on the bridge between the yes and no sides of the question. And thinking about it was driving her mad.

The day before with Jim, after those first initial tense moments, had been wonderful but all day she'd caught glimpses of him looking at her with the saddest expression in his eyes. He'd always quickly masked his inner thoughts, but she'd finally put a name to it. Longing. As if he were on the outside looking in.

He must have spent much of his life feeling that way. When other men picked up their children from Sunday school classes and went home with their

wives, Jim stayed behind. Alone. Even when he went
for dinner to the homes of his church members he left
alone. From the stories he'd shared with her over
lunches at the church, she gathered that his childhood
had apparently been much the same. Though hers had
been more than a little messed up and often mired in
pretense, at least she'd had a family. So now, not only
was she conflicted about his proposal, she felt guilty.

Guilty for withholding the family he'd admitted to
needing. Guilty for not jumping at the chance to give
Ian the full-time mother and father he craved. And
guilty for not saying yes and putting her future in the
Lord's hands as the wife of one of His most steadfast
servants.

And all because she was afraid to give up control.
That was the barrier she was afraid to cross. Until
she'd left Jim and been forced to rely solely on herself, she'd never had control of her own destiny. It
had been frightening, but it had been exhilarating too
and later, safe. No one could hurt her or disappoint
her if she relied on no one but herself. So who was
she afraid would disappoint her? Jim? Or God?

"Come along, Ian." Holly shouted above the telly,
unable to go forward in her thinking. Today's activity
would be her solace. Later she would just have to find
the courage to do what she had to do, because with
every passing minute, her mind was inching ever
closer to her heart's desire.

Jim grabbed hold of the beam, muscles straining
against the enormous weight of one of the major

pieces of the timber framing. He and the other men bore it directly to the pickup for delivery to the new site up by the church. There was another crew up there to do the unloading so it was time for his team to take a break.

He stepped back from the truck as it pulled away and accepted a sport bottle full of water from one of the men. After walking into the shade, he pulled off his ball cap and took a couple of swigs of the water. When that failed to cool him off, he twisted off the cap and dumped the rest of the icy water over his head. It felt wonderful.

"Now there's an idea for cooling off," Trent called out as he sauntered over. "Hey, look around at this site. This would be a great place to put the pastorate. There's good drainage with the land still falling away on the other side of the meadow. Plus it has a great view sitting up high like this."

Jim nodded. "Yeah, it'd be a good place," he said absently, his mind drifting to Holly once again.

Trent stared at him for a few seconds. "I'm going to grab another bottle of water. Let me know if you want to talk about it."

"Yeah," he promised with a wry smile. He couldn't seem to hide a thing from Trent anymore. Still, Jim knew he wouldn't tell Trent what had him so preoccupied today. Because only God could help him. It was all in His hands now.

Jim leaned against what had to be a century-old oak tree and surveyed the work as the men took a break. A few more roof trusses had to be knocked apart and the second-story work would be done.

He pushed away from the tree, too unsettled to just stand around waiting. He moved toward the building, wanting to get back at it, but he knew the men needed the break. With nothing to do, Jim's mind still drifted to the scene at the house and the decision Holly had promised to give him tomorrow.

No matter how hard he tried to give his anxiety to God and rest in Him, Jim was still afraid that he'd made a grave error. He'd thought the Lord had spoken to him. That was why he'd taken Holly to the house to propose. Why else would the solution to his worries have appeared as if from nowhere? He hadn't even known Trent and Maggie still had that house. It had seemed like an answer. But now he wasn't so sure.

What would he do if Holly said no? The only answer to that one was that he had to fight to keep the door open. It wasn't as if she would suddenly disappear from his life. New York wasn't around the corner, but it wasn't New Zealand, either. He'd still have time to—

Pain and lights suddenly exploded in his skull. Then the world tilted and went black.

The next instant he opened his eyes and stared up at a brilliant white ceiling. He slammed his eyes shut against the brightness and the pain that blasted through his head.

"Well, hello there," a voice said from next to him. "You've decided to join us at last."

Jim turned his head toward the voice and opened his eyes more carefully this time. What was Trudy from the ER doing at the building site? he wondered. Then he remembered having seen a ceiling overhead. "Where am I?"

"Paoli Memorial, Pastor Jim. Let me get the doctor, then I'll go out and tell the men who brought you in that you're awake. They're out there praying their hearts out. You gave a lot of people a big scare today."

"Holly?"

"No, your wife and son weren't with you. It's Mr. Osborne and some others. For once, Mr. Osborne isn't here with one of his kids."

Jim slitted his eyes and opened them more carefully. "Trent's here? Can you get him for me?"

"Doctor first. Friend later. Let me get the doc."

He didn't have time for this. Holly and Ian were coming for a movie. It was his last night. He wanted her to see how terrific their life together could be. He couldn't do that from the hospital. "I want to leave," he said sitting up. The room spun and Trudy had him flat on his back before it settled down.

"Do I need to tie you down?" she teased.

"I'll be good, but I'm not staying."

"We'll see."

She left and a frowning young doctor came in minutes later. "You have a concussion, Mr. Dillon.

We'd like to keep you here for observation. I've requested a room for the—''

"No," Jim said and pushed himself carefully to a sitting position. "I'm not staying."

"Mr. Dillon, I don't think you understand."

"I understand just fine. I'm going home."

"You've been unconscious for over an hour."

Jim knew he probably sounded irrational but he couldn't stay. Tonight was too important. "Look, I'll sign any waiver you want. You won't get sued. I just need to leave."

The doctor shook his head. "We still have to do a neurological workup to make sure your reflexes are okay. I'll get your friend. Perhaps he can talk some sense into you."

The doctor had Jim practically jumping through hoops and grudgingly said there seemed not to be anything more wrong with him than the concussion. Jim stewed. Did they think he was an idiot? He knew what he was doing and how he felt. He looked up when Trent came in. "That do-it-my-way-or-else look isn't going to work," he told his friend. "Get me my shoes and take me home."

"Why are you being so stubborn? We can get along without you for one Sunday."

Jim blinked. Tomorrow was Sunday! He was so wrapped up in worrying about losing Holly, he'd forgotten his responsibilities. "I hadn't even thought about services," he admitted. "It's about Holly and Ian. They were supposed to come over tonight." He hesitated. "Trent, she didn't give me an answer. She asked for time. Till tomorrow. We're supposed to kick back and watch a movie tonight. I wanted her to see how great it would be for us to be together as a family just doing an ordinary family thing. Tonight's my last night to convince her. I can't do that from a hospital bed. Now are you going to hand me my sneakers and take me home or am I going to have to walk?''

Chapter Fifteen

"This has me really nervous," Trent said stopping in the doorway that led to the rest of the building from Jim's rooms.

"Maggie needs you now that Holly dropped your kids off. Mickey said she and Ian left ten minutes ago. What can happen to me on my own sofa in the next few minutes?"

Trent glared. "How about you could start exhibiting that list of symptoms I'm supposed to watch for?"

Jim took a deep breath. "Then Holly will see them and do whatever she's supposed to do. It's all written down. You're giving me a headache."

"No, I'm not. A log twelve inches in diameter whacked you on the head and gave you that headache."

"The last thing I remember is hoisting a beam into the truck with you and about five other guys," Jim sighed and closed his eyes. He really was feeling nauseated, but he didn't want Trent staying when Maggie needed him.

"That's because you have a concussion and amnesia. You lost about the ten, maybe fifteen minutes before the accident."

Jim thought of his buddy Joshua who'd lost almost his first thirty years of memories. Now that was amnesia! Ten minutes he could live with. "I'm fine. Go home to your wife and kiddies."

"Okay. I hope you know what you're doing. I'll lock up the front of the church and put a note on the door to send Holly and Ian around here."

"Thanks, Trent. I'll be fine. Really."

"You'd better be or untold numbers of people are going to be mighty unhappy with me."

"Go," Jim groaned and wondered if his voice had just sounded odd. No. He was just tired was all. He'd never had a headache this bad. It felt as if his skull were coming apart at the seams. He closed his eyes. He wasn't going to go to sleep. He'd just rest his eyes.

Holly pulled up in front of the lovely old barn Jim loved so much. "Here we are, poppet. Run ahead and make sure the front door's open for me will you?" she asked, her eyes widening at how tremulous her voice sounded. She prayed for calm. Jim was a wonderful man. And soon he'd be her husband. Again.

"Are you all right, Mum?"

"I'm fine," she said and smiled. "Let's get dinner into the fridge and get set to surprise your father."

"He really is going to be surprised about dinner. He's always talking about how much he loves your steak-and-kidney pie."

"I hope so. I just wish it hadn't taken two hours to find lamb kidneys. Who would have thought it could take so long? I hope he hasn't been worried."

Holly bent to pull the bags out of the back seat when she heard Ian call to her. "Mum, there's a note that says we should go round back to Dad's outside door. I'll go get him to open up. It's closer to the kitchen this way."

"Right-o. I'll just wait here," Holly told him and sank to the seat. She had to be out of her mind planning to cook a full meal after chasing five energetic children over hill and dale all day. She was afraid they'd enjoyed rolling down the hills and climbing the redoubts of Valley Forge more than the historical sites and artifacts they'd seen. But it had been a good day and after a few minutes rest, it would be just as good an evening.

"Mum! Mum!" Ian screamed, tears running down his face. "Come quick. There's something wrong with Dad!"

"What? What's wrong?"

"He's sick or something. He was throwing up in the bathroom and he stumbled and almost fell when he got up off the floor. He can't even talk right."

Holly's stomach turned to lead. He wouldn't! He couldn't be drinking. He just couldn't! She looked at Ian's tear-stained face. *How could you have put him in this position?*

"You stay here, poppet. I'll go check on your father."

"But I want to help."

"Ian, stay here. Do you hear me? Sit right there in that seat and don't move! I'll be back as soon as I know what's wrong with him."

Holly half ran, half stalked. "Jim, where are you?" she called on entering the sitting room. She turned toward a noise and watched him stagger out of the bathroom. He had to grab hold of the doorway to keep from falling. "I'm nod feelin' too good. I sink you bedder help me get back to the couch."

Holly stared in horror at the specter from the past as he wove a step or two toward her. It felt as if he'd just thrust a knife into her heart. He was drunk. So stinking drunk he couldn't even stand without holding onto something. She backed away, fury replacing the pain.

"How could you do this? How could you let your son see you this way? You promised me. And I warned you. No second chances. You won't get near him again. He'll be out of the country before morning!"

"Mum! Don't talk to him like that!"

Holly wheeled toward Ian who stood just inside the door. "I told you to stay at the car."

"He's sick. Can't you see he's sick?"

"I'm sorry, Ian. I should never have trusted him. He's not sick. He's been drinking."

"No! Can't you see?"

"Come on, Ian. We're leaving."

"Holly!" Jim yelled. "I'm not drinkin' again. And I won't let you take him. Not this time. This time I don't deserve it."

Jim stumbled and caught the back of the sofa. His head pounded and the room spun. He watched in horror, his heart turning to stone in his chest as Holly faded from sight through the open doorway. His legs felt like jelly. He had to stop her but the room spun unmercifully. He fell just trying to get around the edge of the couch.

He had no choice but to stay there on the floor and pray that God would find a way to stop her from taking Ian out of his life. He no longer knew if he wanted Holly in it. How could she think he'd turn away from all he held dear to drink again? What did she think he'd find in a bottle that the Lord hadn't given him?

It's for the best, he told himself. It was clear that he'd have spent his whole life proving himself and still she'd never have really trusted him. He just wished the truth didn't hurt so much.

At Paradise Found, Ian tore out of the car and turned to face Holly, when she pulled in next to the carriage house. "I won't go! I'll tell them at the airport you're kidnapping me!"

"Ian, get inside now. You'll thank me one day."

"I won't thank you because I hate you!" He turned and ran for the woods. Mickey and Rachel and Daniel would help him fix it. They had to.

Ian could hardly breathe by the time he got to the playhouse. "Help," he gasped, trying to pull himself up the ladder. He was afraid he wouldn't make it, but then his mates were there, grabbing his arms and dragging him inside.

"Where's your inhaler?" Rachel demanded.

He felt Mickey patting his pockets. "Here! Ian, here it is. I shook it. It's ready to use." Mickey helped him sit up and held the inhaler to his mouth. After the second hit, Ian could tell right away that the medicine was working. It would be okay this time. He knew getting upset wouldn't help, so he closed his eyes the way Dad told him and took some deep breaths.

Ian blinked back tears. His dad had helped him so much with his last attack and when his dad needed it, Ian hadn't helped him at all. "My dad's sick."

"Yeah, our dad said a humongous log hit Pastor Jim in the head and knocked him right out. Bam! Flat out on the ground," Daniel told him with rather ghoulish enthusiasm. "And then they took him to the hospital in the back of a pickup and he never woke up the whole way there. Then when he did wake up, he made Dad take him home 'cause you and your mom were coming. Dad said he was being pigheaded. That means—"

"I know what it means." He didn't have time for Daniel and his weirdness. "My mom says he was drinking and she's taking me back to New Zealand. We have to do something!"

"Drinking?" Rachel asked.

"Beer and wine and stuff like that."

"Pastor Jim wouldn't do that," Mickey said. "We'll get our dad to tell her about the log and it'll be okay."

Oh, if only it was that easy, but Ian was very afraid it was much more complicated with his parents. "I don't think so. She wrecked it. Dad was really mad. Even though he sounded kind of funny like he could hardly talk, he looked even madder than he did the other day at us when we locked them in the closet. He shouted at her!"

"Pastor Jim shouted?" Rachel asked. Her big brown eyes were all wide and shocked.

"Uh-oh. This *is* bad," Mickey decreed. "Pastor Jim never shouts."

"Yeah, really bad," Daniel agreed.

Rachel folded her arms. "I have an idea."

Daniel rolled his eyes. "Oh, great. Like the last one? Oh," Daniel squeaked in a high voice, "it'll be so romantic if we lock them in the closet."

"The closet was your idea, dummy. I just agreed with you."

"I'm just a kid! If I told you to jump off a cliff, would you?"

"This isn't getting us anywhere, people," Mickey snapped. "Rachel, what's this idea?"

"We run away."

Daniel crossed his arms and frowned. "I'm not running away, Dad promised to make pizza for dinner. And I get all mosquito bit if I'm out at night."

"Then you go tell Dad about Pastor Jim being

alone. It sounded like he needs someone to take care of him. I think Mrs. Dillon was supposed to watch that he didn't throw up and stuff."

"But he did!" Ian gasped. "And he could hardly walk."

"Go tell Dad, Daniel," Mickey ordered, "and don't forget the Kids' Club pledge."

Daniel crawled to the ladder. "I know. A secret's a secret and anyone who reveals a secret is dead meat! You know that really *is* a dumb saying. I mean, it's not called meat if it's not dead."

Ian thought he'd scream. "Please just go! My dad could be dying!"

"I'm goin'. I'm goin'," Daniel groused as he disappeared from sight.

"I'm not sure they'll buy us running away because Ian's parents had a fight," Mickey began. "Him running away, yeah. But us? And where would we go?"

"You won't be included. You come back here in a while when they can't find us and find the note. Ian and I do the running away."

"You and Ian? I can't let you do that. You could get hurt if I'm not there to protect you."

"Take it from me. This will work out perfect," Rachel assured him.

"That's what you said about the closet idea," Mickey reminded her.

"You know," Ian said. "I think locking them in there worked till today. Mom was really excited about going to Dad's tonight. She was even going to make him steak-and-kidney pie, because he loves it, and hasn't had it since they were married."

Mickey sighed. "But this is risky, people. Really risky. Rach, you know Dad shut down Operation Wedding Ring after the closet thing. They could get a lot madder than they did about that."

"Do either one of you have a better idea?" Rachel demanded.

He and Mickey looked at each other then they both shook their heads.

"Okay, then," Rachel said. "Now about the note and where Ian and I will go..."

Holly wiped her eyes and started down the step, dragging the heavy suitcase behind her. She had to stop crying. Half the clothes she'd packed were probably damp with tears. Nothing had ever hurt this much. Not even Jim's many betrayals during their marriage. It was worse this time because she felt cut off from not only Jim but Ian and God, as well. And to be drunk in the church he claimed to love so dearly. Why would he do this?

"What are you doing here?" Trent Osborne's voice cracked in the silence of the oppressive summer evening.

Holly pulled the heavy suitcase toward the open trunk. "I'm righting a wrong. I should never have come here. I should never have believed in him."

"Who? Jim?"

"Yes. Your friend the drunken pastor who's even

now falling all over the church looking like some sort of street bum.''

"Drunken past—'' Trent's eyes widened. "Tell me what you saw.''

Holly sniffed. "I sent Ian to get him. He came back saying Jim was vomiting and couldn't walk. I went round the back and he was staggering out of the bath. He not only could hardly stand, he could scarcely talk.''

"Come on. I'll drive. We have to get over there.''

Confused Holly just stared at him. Did he expect her to go with him while he confronted Jim? "Why would I want to see him again?''

"He wasn't drinking, Holly,'' Trent all but growled. "He got hit on the head with one of the big header beams when it broke loose prematurely. He's got a concussion and wouldn't stay in the hospital because he didn't want to chance messing up your nice little family night at home. You were supposed to be there any minute to take care of him or I'd never have left him alone.''

Holly felt all the blood drain from her head. What had she done? She grabbed onto the top of the open car door to steady herself. "He's hurt?''

"Maybe a lot worse than we thought or I never would have let him sign himself out. Are you coming?''

Holly hesitated, remembering the fury in Jim's eyes when she left him. He might not want her there. "Yes, I'm coming.'' She had to know that he was all right.

It took less time than usual to get to the Tabernacle because Trent drove a bit like a madman, taking turns on the empty country roads as if he were driving a sports car instead of a two-ton pickup. Holly prayed the whole way there. Not for her own safety but Jim's.

She also faced what she had really done. She had thrown the gift of Jim's love, which the Lord had given her, back in His face and Jim's. She had chosen instead to allow her own past experience with her mother to color the present and future. And worse yet, in wresting control of her destiny from God's hand, she had destroyed it and possibly Jim, as well.

Trent didn't waste time parking in front but hopped the curb at the handicap ramps and drove around the back of the building. Jim's door was still sitting open. They found him sitting on the floor, with his head propped against the arm of the settee.

Holly stood paralyzed near the door. How could she have left him like this? *I'm so sorry, Lord. I deserve to lose him. But please let him be all right and let him forgive me.*

"You don't look real comfortable," Trent told him.

"Can't fall off the floor." Jim didn't open his eyes. "Anybody get the number of that truck?"

Trent chuckled and went down on one knee next to Jim. "I think it was beam PR2. Do you know what that means?"

"Joins P and R. Second truss from front. Why?"

"I figured if you remembered that, I could dispense with 'What's your name, what day is it and where are you?' But I still think I'd better take you back to the hospital. You should have stayed there instead of trying to keep a date with Holly.''

"I don't want to talk about Holly," Jim growled.

"She's here," Trent whispered, but Holly still heard.

Jim's eyes snapped open. He flinched then searched the room for her. "Go away," he snarled.

"I'm sorry. I didn't know you'd been hurt."

"Well, you should have known I wasn't drunk. Go away."

Holly felt as if he'd torn her heart out. Somehow she held back her tears. "I—I can't. Trent drove."

"And Trent's driving again," Trent said, boosting Jim up off the floor. "Come on, buddy boy, we're off to the ER and this time you stay put."

"Sure. Why not? Isn't like I have anyone to hurry home for this time."

Holly put her hand to her chest. Surely her heart was bleeding in there. She followed the two men. When Trent stopped to get a better grip around Jim's waist, she reached out to take the keys Jim had attached to his belt loop. He flinched away and drilled her with an accusing stare. "Leave me alone. Just leave me alone."

"I—I thought you'd want your door locked."

For the first time she saw something flicker in his eyes that had nothing to do with anger. "Yeah. Thanks." He looked away and fumbled for the keys. His frightening lack of coordination made the simple task difficult. He finally handed them to her carefully, as if to avoid her touch.

Trent had helped him into the front seat by the time she got to the vehicle. "I'll stay here," she told them after handing Jim the keys just as carefully.

"No, you won't," Trent said. "I'm not leaving you here with no car and nowhere to go. Just get in so we can get him there."

"But he doesn't want me there."

Trent's cell phone rang. He sighed, grabbed it out of his shirt pocket and flipped it open. "Yeah?" His eyes widened in alarm. "What? Are you sure? How about the playhouse? Mag, try to calm down. This isn't good for the baby. Wait a second while I flip this to speaker and fill these guys in."

Holly already expected the worst but when Trent glanced at each of them, she knew it was Ian.

"It seems that Ian and Rachel have run away," he told them. "Apparently Ian went out to the playhouse all upset, threatening to run away so he wouldn't have to leave the country."

Maggie's voice sounded nearly as frantic as Holly's heartbeat as she continued. "They left a note. It says he's going to seek political asylum!" Maggie half laughed, half sobbed. "It would be really funny if we knew where they are. Holly, do you think Ian would know where to go to do something like this?"

"He'd know to go to a federal building. Where's the nearest one?"

"Philly. In Center City," Trent said.

"Would Ian know how to get to Center City? And does he have money?" Maggie wanted to know.

Holly felt as if her legs had turned to jelly. She'd been so happy less than two hours ago. And now her faithlessness had wreaked havoc in one family and destroyed the promise of a second.

"I gave each of them money today. I don't know how much they had left after buying souvenirs. But I'm afraid that combined with what he took with him today it could be enough to get them as far as Philadelphia. But even if they knew where to go and how to go about getting there, I doubt a federal building would be open to the public at this time on a Saturday."

"What does Mickey say about all this?" Trent asked Maggie.

"He says he went to tell Holly what Ian said about running away but that he'd seen her in the truck when you pulled out of the drive. Then he went back to the clubhouse and the kids were gone. And of course Daniel had already come to tell us Jim was alone so he doesn't know anything at all."

"They don't have much of a head start," Trent said and Holly tried to take solace in that, but they were so little. "Call the state police," he continued, "and I'll be there after I drop Jim at the ER."

"Forget it," Jim said. "Take me over to your place. I'm fine. A lot better."

"Jim, please," Holly begged. She didn't know what she'd do if anything happened to him. And now with Ian missing she was sure to lose her mind worrying about both of them. "Let him take you to the—"

"Ian's my son, too," he told Trent, ignoring her as if she weren't there. "If you don't take me there, I'll take a cab to Paradise Found. Besides which, it's way out of your way and Maggie shouldn't be alone at a time like this."

Trent shook his head. "Anybody ever tell you that you have a head like a rock?"

"Yeah, that's why I'm so good at banging my head against walls. Soon or later, though, even *I* learn to recognize a futile cause when I see it. Let's get a move on."

Chapter Sixteen

Jim gingerly put his head back against the headrest of Trent's front seat and took deep breaths, trying to ignore the motion and Holly's nearness next to him. He didn't have to look to know that she was still in the same position she'd been in since sliding into the truck. She sat with her head bent, her hair hanging down to screen her face. And though she hadn't made a sound, he knew she was crying.

He didn't want to be so in tune with her that he knew by instinct alone what she felt. And he certainly didn't want to care. If she was frightened for Ian and feeling guilty, it was her own fault. She should feel guilty. If it weren't for her suspicion and faithlessness, Ian would be safe back at the Tabernacle lying on the floor, eating popcorn and watching a movie. If it weren't for her, he wouldn't be sitting there feeling as if the heart had been ripped out of him.

The truck rocked as Trent pulled into his long drive and Jim forced himself to ease his eyes open. And the reality that Ian and Rachel were in danger slapped him in the face.

In front of the house sat four police cars. Even the state police, with all their weighty responsibilities, realized the seriousness of two young children missing. And they'd clearly called in extra help.

He, for one, felt like a miserable failure of a parent even though, and frankly because, he'd only been one for a little more than two months. Jim felt Holly tense.

"Oh, Ian," she whispered under her breath.

Jim fought the urge to wrap her in his arms to give and receive comfort. He wanted neither because clearly it was wrong to want Holly to be part of his life. He wished it didn't cut like a knife.

Trent drove past the police cruisers around to the back of the house, parking behind the family van. "Jim, do you think Holly can help you get inside? I really have to get to Maggie."

"Go. I'm worried about her, too. I'll be fine."

"Thanks," Trent said over his shoulder and was gone in a flash, leaving them alone.

"Jim, I'm—"

"Don't, Holly." He was surprised the way his voice cracked like a whip in the truck cab. He sighed. "Just leave it alone. Please. Ian and Rachel are all I'm up to dealing with right now. Let's just go inside and see what the police have to say. The rest will wait."

Holly got out and ran around the truck. She pulled

open the door before he could even find the handle. And blocked his way. "There's one thing that won't wait," she said looking up at him with eyes reddened from crying.

Some women looked awful when they cried, but could Holly at least cooperate in that area? No. Holly looked beautifully tragic with her emerald eyes swimming in a sea of tears and her cheeks flushed. When their gazes met, his heart tripped, which only seconds before he would have said was impossible. He'd thought that surely there was now only a hole in the middle of his chest where his heart should be.

"I apologize for doubting you and for jumping to conclusions. My only excuse is that I've been so frightened to give up control over my life to you. And today I'd decided that I had to or I'd never be truly happy. Then I walked in on what looked like my worst nightmare come true. I didn't stop to think. I just reacted. And I'll be sorry for it for the rest of my life."

A pain speared through his head. Jim winced and put his hand to brow. "I can't deal with this now."

"You don't need to," she said, her voice choked.

When she put her hand on his arm, her touch seemed to burn him and instinct alone made him flinch from her. He hadn't tried to hurt her, but she drew a sharp breath as if he had.

"I don't expect you to accept my apology, Jim, but I had to say it. So now I did and I guess we'd better get you inside. I'm sorry I have to be the one to help you. I can see you don't want me touching you but I'm afraid you'll need my help just the same.''

Jim wished it was true. But he'd only flinched because her touch reminded him of all he'd lost. So when she wrapped her slender arm about his waist and eased against him, he closed his eyes trying to memorize the feel of holding her close for the lonely years ahead.

Unfortunately, even with Holly steadying him, the world still tilted crazily as they walked toward the house. By the time she got him up the couple steps to the porch and across it to the back door, his knees had gone from feeling like Jell-O to having all the stability of water.

One of the officers ran to the door and grabbed him. "I think you belong in a hospital, sir."

Jim sighed. He'd never really had a mother and today everyone wanted the job. "I'm just a little unsteady on my feet, officer," he said as he sank into a chair at the kitchen table.

Jim saw the looks the three officers standing in the big country kitchen passed among themselves, but he ignored them. It was *his* son who was missing, and Jim intended to be there to lend whatever help he could to the search.

Just then a fourth officer gave a cursory knock on the door and opened it. He entered and turned his attention to Maggie. "I found the tree house, ma'am. Like your son said, they weren't there, but I did find this. Does one of your children have asthma?"

Behind him Holly gasped for breath as she reached

for the inhaler. "It's my son's," she said then Jim felt her other hand come to rest on his shoulder. "Our son's," she corrected herself. "He's a severe asthmatic. He can't be without it."

The cops exchanged glances. Jim couldn't tell if they thought Holly was being a hysterical mother or if they understood her near panic. "Ma'am, I'm sure they haven't gone far."

"Officers," Jim said, wondering if indeed they understood the seriousness of the situation, "my son is not from this area. He's here for experimental treatment because his asthma is so severe. And in case you really believe they won't go far, Ian found his way across New York City several weeks ago to hear me speak. He'd only seen the church once on a bus ride with his mother. He's quite capable of figuring out how to reach Center City and he has a very bright little girl, who *does* know the area, with him. Have you alerted the transit police to keep a lookout?"

The cops looked suddenly worried. "Yes, sir. We did it as a precaution. Brian, why don't you inform Philly and the two township forces between here and the train about the kids. Then look around that carriage house over there. Are there current photos of them, folks?"

"There's one I took of the two of them together on the Fourth," Trent said and hurried from the room to get it.

"Mrs. Osborne, I know you searched the house but I wonder if we could take one more look."

"Go ahead. Look anywhere you want. I just want them back safely."

"Yes, ma'am," the officer said. Both men dropped their big Smokey-the-Bear-like hats on the kitchen counter and went off on their search. "Jerry, you take the second and third floor. I'll take the basement and this one," the sergeant said as they left the kitchen.

"I feel so guilty, Maggie," Jim said and reached out to take her hand. "This has to be Ian's doing."

She squeezed his hand in return. "Oh, don't be so sure. It's probably even partly Trent's and my fault." She pulled her hand back and ran both her hands through her hair.

Maggie looked a tad guilty suddenly and as if the weight of the kids' disappearance rested on her shoulders alone. "They have a club. It's called the Kids' Club. They think we don't know but I heard them plotting to get a kitten right after their first Christmas with us." Her smile was wistful. "We thought it was good for them to pull together that way after all the upheaval they'd had in their lives. I even put off caving in on the kitten issue for a long time just to watch them trying to get around me.

"After Holly arrived, we got the idea that they were trying to throw you two together. It was confirmed by my mother when she overheard them plotting in one of the guest bedrooms on the Fourth. It seemed harmless, and quite frankly a good idea, so we let it ride. But then they locked you two in that closet. Trent told our four kids in no uncertain terms that Operation Wedding Ring had been busted.

"Now I'm afraid we let it go on too long. Ian ran to his cohorts in crime today instead of telling one of us that Holly had misunderstood what she'd seen. Believe me, the only thing about this stunt that doesn't smack of our kids is Rachel being the one who went with him."

Jim looked over his shoulder at Holly. She was positively stricken.

"Operation Wedding Ring?" she asked.

"That's what they called it," Maggie said.

"Did you know about this?" Holly asked him.

"No. What I *thought* had developed between us had nothing to do with Ian."

"It *did* develop and it was wonderful," she whispered for his ears only, then turned away and went out to the back porch.

Jim wanted to enjoy seeing her hurt, but it only served to hurt him more. And that just wasn't fair! This whole mess was her fault. From the time he'd found her again, he'd accepted the entire blame for the breakup of their marriage. He hadn't let her take any responsibility for what had gone wrong between them. But this time he'd done nothing wrong.

"Well, that was lovely of you," Maggie snapped, her brown eyes narrowing in annoyance. Her reaction made his stomach roll. He closed his eyes, breathing slowly against the nausea. Why did she think he was being unfair?

Jim looked at her again. "Please, not now. Lecture me later if you have to. Do you think you could share a little of that flat cola you've been sipping for the last couple of months?''

Maggie nodded and stood. "You should be in a hospital.''

"Another candidate,'' he grumbled.

"Candidate?'' Maggie asked as she plunked down the soda.

"For the job of my mother. A nurse, a doctor, Trent, Holly and one state police officer have apparently applied for the job. So far, though, you're the most qualified.'' His stomach flipped again. He groaned. "How do you stand feeling like this?''

Maggie smiled, if a little sadly. "I know I'll get to have a baby to hold when this is all over, and I'm told the nausea shouldn't last much longer.''

Both officers returned then with Trent. "Nothing,'' Trent said on a sigh. "I guess it was too much to hope for. We've decided against putting this on the TV stations for a little while longer. Sergeant Mosby thinks as it gets further toward dark they might get scared and come home on their own.''

"You think they might?'' Maggie asked the officers who were putting on their hats.

"You'd be surprised how many kids go home because of an owl hooting. The night sounds start and most kids this age rethink the wisdom of their actions. We're going to roll now and start patrolling the roads between here and the two nearest train stations. Let us know if the kids call and we'll certainly let you know if anyone picks them up.''

Holly came back in as the officers left. Far from looking better, she looked even more devastated.

Jim clenched his teeth. *I don't want to care, Lord.*

"...so I'll wait in the apartment," she was saying to Maggie and Trent when Jim realized Holly was speaking. "I'm sure it would make you all more comfortable. I just wanted you to know how sorry I am that my stupid actions have involved Rachel."

"Don't you dare leave!" Maggie cried and went over to hug Holly. "We don't blame you. This was a lot of people's fault and we'd all feel terrible if you were over there worrying alone. You get in here and sit down with us."

Jim wanted to tell Maggie not to speak for him. Then he looked over at Trent and saw his own anger reflected in his friend's eyes. It bothered him. It made him mad. But why? He wanted his friends on his side, didn't he? He wanted them to share his feelings as well as understanding them.

But is being angry at Holly really being on your side? a traitorous voice whispered from the vicinity of his heart.

He studiously ignored that voice. It was all her fault. She hadn't trusted him and her threats had sent two children out into the world trying to fix what she'd destroyed.

Holly dropped into the seat Maggie pointed to at the table. They'd all sat there before, but that night there had been camaraderie and laughter. She wondered if any of them would ever laugh again.

What if something happens to the children? There are such terrible people out there in the world. Oh please, God. Please protect them.

A knock at the back door interrupted her dark study. Trent opened it. "Sir," the voice said. "We're paramedics from Paoli Memorial. The state police asked us to stop and take a look at a concussion victim."

"Come on in. Old hard-head's in here. He's the one wearing the death-warmed-up look on his face."

Maggie stood and held out her hand to Holly. "Come help me get something for the kids to eat. Trent, why not drag old hard-head into the family room so these nice gentlemen can have more room to take a look at him."

Trent returned to the kitchen a few minutes later. He'd helped Jim into the adjacent family room. She could tell he was still angry with her, but that was okay. She was glad Jim had good friends.

She and Maggie shredded cheese for the pizza as Trent worked the dough he'd made earlier in the day, before she tore all their worlds apart. If only she'd seen Trent before she'd seen Jim. If only he'd stayed in the hospital where he probably belonged. If only she'd had enough faith in him and in God.

"We're hungry," Daniel said, stomping into the room.

"Yeah. Hungry," Gracie parroted.

"When's dinner going to be ready?" Mickey asked as he came into the room a few seconds later.

"Aren't you at all worried about Rachel?" Trent asked them.

Mickey shrugged. "I told her this was a dumb idea. It's her head."

"Rachel's a big girl," Grace pronounced.

"She knows what she's doing," Daniel told them. "Rachel's smart. Just don't tell her I said so."

Trent gave Maggie an odd look. "Will you clear the table and set it for dinner, kids?" Trent asked, his voice as odd as the look he'd shot Maggie. "Have you got any idea why Mickey's so calm about this?" he asked Maggie.

Maggie frowned. "He has been since he found them gone and brought back the note. Do you think he knows more than he's said?"

"Possibly. Did you call all their friends' parents?"

"No. After reading the note, that never occurred to me."

"Are you up to watching the pizza and feeding these three? If the paramedics don't cart him off to the hospital, Jim and I can call their friends' homes. I'll use my cell phone and Jim can use the kitchen portable."

"But then all our friends will know what Rachel's doing. This could get embarrassing," Daniel said.

"Embarrassing? Daniel, your sister and Ian are missing," Holly told him.

Daniel shrugged and sauntered back toward the table as if he didn't have a care in the world.

Trent leaned between them. "I smell a rat," he

growled softly. "We'll start making those calls after the paramedics leave."

Mickey appeared at her side as Maggie and Trent went off to look in on Jim and the paramedics. Now he looked worried. "Why are paramedics here? Is Pastor Jim really hurt that bad?"

Holly was surprised by his attitude about Jim when he was so cavalier about Rachel and Ian having run away. "Yes, I'm afraid he is," she told him truthfully, "but he won't go to the hospital. If you know where Ian and Rachel have gone, please let us know. Maybe then Jim will go to the hospital where he belongs."

"You're worried about him!" Mickey blurted out, excited and a bit too thrilled. "I thought you were mad at him."

Holly remembered Operation Wedding Ring. She guessed he felt he had a vested interest in their relationship. Maybe if she reassured Mickey about Ian's future, he'd tell them where the children had gone if he knew. "I was wrong to be angry. I wish I could let Ian know that I won't take him back to New Zealand no matter what happens with me and his father."

"Ian wants you guys to get married," Daniel said having materialized on the other side of her.

"I'm afraid he's doomed to be disappointed then. Pastor Jim is very angry at me. He has every right because I mistrusted him. But that doesn't mean that we don't both love Ian very much. Sometimes adults just can't work out their differences."

"But you could try. Mom and Dad did," Mickey told her.

Holly smiled sadly. "It isn't my call, boys. And Pastor Jim seems pretty unmovable on the subject just now." The boys looked at each other and went back to the table. Holly watched them set three places, but they didn't even glance at each other, so there was no way she could read anything into their actions.

And there was always the possibility that they didn't know anything after all.

Chapter Seventeen

Forty-five minutes after they arrived, the paramedics left and pronounced that it was indeed safe for Jim to remain at Maggie and Trent's. However, if his symptoms worsened at all, he was to be taken to the hospital immediately. Jim and Trent then called the home of every child the Osborne children came in contact with. No one had seen Rachel or Ian.

The adults settled around the kitchen table again after cleaning up after dinner. No one had been in the least hungry but Holly and Trent had forced themselves to eat. Maggie and Jim continued to sip flat cola. "I still think Mickey and Daniel know more than they're saying," Trent said as he settled next to Maggie.

"Why do you think that?" Holly asked.

"Because if we have a problem with Mickey, it's that he takes too much responsibility toward everything, especially his brother and sisters. After the accident that killed Michael and Sarah, Mickey was paralyzed. We'd been assured that he would walk again but Mickey thought differently for a variety of reasons. He was afraid to be a burden and put a strain on Maggie's and my iffy relationship. He tried to get us to put him in an institution, thinking we'd find it easier to take care of his brother and sisters if he weren't around to add to our work."

Maggie picked up the story. "Even after we brought him home and were a solid family, we nearly had to force him to be a kid again. His attitude toward his sister taking off like this just doesn't fit with Mickey's personality."

"And Daniel's afraid of the dark," Jim added. "He never even flinched when I said that pretty soon they'd be out there alone in the dark."

"Is he really?" Holly asked. "I wasn't sure after hearing that locking us in the closet wasn't an accident." She smiled sadly, remembering the machinations of all the children that day. "I'd gladly stay in there for a whole day if I could relive this one."

Jim sucked in a sharp breath. Did it bother him hearing she was sorry? Perhaps he doubted her sincerity the way she'd once doubted his. Had he felt this helpless, wanting more of their relationship, yet unable to prove he would never willingly fail her again? And was he now feeling the way she had—desperately wanting to trust but so afraid to take the chance that it hurt?

"How long till dark?" Maggie asked, drawing Holly out of her musings.

Jim glanced at his watch. "About an hour."

Unable to sit still any longer, Holly got up to finish the few things in the kitchen they'd left undone. She wiped the counters on one side of the kitchen, then started on the other side. Frowning, she picked up the last pizza pan. It was empty, and she was sure there'd been four pieces left. She shrugged. I guess Maggie wrapped them up, she thought absently and washed the pan.

"Where do you keep the pizza pans?" she called toward the table.

"Oh, I'm sorry. I forgot to wrap up the leftovers."

Holly frowned. "I thought you had."

Maggie stood. "No. Trent, did you?"

Trent shook his head.

"Don't look at me. I could hardly watch them eat it let alone get close enough to wrap it up," Jim admitted.

"Well, somebody did something with it," Maggie groused and went to the refrigerator. She moved several things then emerged with a frown on her face. "It's not here."

"Where's Ian's inhaler?" Jim asked suddenly. "Holly, didn't you leave it on the table?" It was the first time he'd talked to her directly since she'd come back in the kitchen after the police left.

"I left it right there where you're sitting."

Trent got up. "I asked the kids to clear the table. Maybe I smell more than one rat. Mickey, Daniel,

Gracie. Come down here please,'' he called up the back stairs that led from the kitchen to the second floor.

They appeared, the second kid in their Kids' Club absent and presumed missing. ''What happened to Ian's inhaler?'' Trent asked, frowning down at the children.

''Inhaler?'' they asked as if they'd never heard of one. However, the three children all knew exactly what it was and how to use it. Holly had shown them in case Ian ever needed their help with it.

''It was on the table. It's bright orange. You couldn't have missed it,'' Jim said.

Daniel shrugged. Mickey shrugged. Gracie shrugged. Trent looked at them then glanced significantly at each adult. ''Okay. In case you hear barking and howling, I wanted you to know that we're asking the police to call in the dogs.''

''It's getting dark. We can't wait any longer,'' Jim added gravely.

Dogs? Holly thought. She didn't remembered talk of dogs.

''I'll get Cindy, Rachel's doll. Holly, you get something of Ian's,'' Maggie ordered.

''Okay,'' Holly said playing along with whatever charade the others were engaged in. She didn't think it was doing any good, then she looked at little Gracie. Gracie looked terrified.

''What will the dogs do?'' the little girl asked.

''They'll sniff what Ian and Rachel smell like from

their things and track them from the tree house to wherever they went,'' Trent told her.

Gracie's brown eyes widened to the size of saucers. ''You can't let them come in the house, Daddy! They might eat my kitty.''

''Of course they won't,'' Daniel said. ''Why would the dogs come in here? They ran *away*.''

''Can we go now?'' Mickey asked quickly.

''Sure. Go on ahead,'' Trent told them, and the kids ran up the back steps toward their rooms. He stood there watching them disappear upward.

''Well, that got us nowhere,'' Maggie declared.

''Grace looked awful worried about her kitty,'' Jim said. ''Are you sure they couldn't be hiding in the house somewhere?''

''I don't know where they could be. But did you catch that little inflection when Daniel said they'd run *away*,'' Trent asked. ''Excuse me. I think I'll reconnoiter the situation.''

Jim put his head in his hands and leaned his elbows on the table. He didn't know how much longer he could hold on to his anger at Holly while watching her suffer. *Oh, please, dear Lord. Let Trent be on to something*, Jim prayed. It was the first time he'd been able to pray since learning Ian was missing.

He was deeply disturbed. All evening, for the first time since finding Him, Jim had been unable to reach out to his Lord. The only way that would make any sense was if his anger had come between them the same way it now stood between him and Holly.

Did that mean his anger wasn't justified? he wondered.

"Look who I found," Trent said, stepping into the room from the dining room.

Jim looked up at Trent, and Trent's expression looked like the personification of thunder. Then Jim looked down at the heads under Trent's big hands. Ian and Rachel stood looking appropriately thunderstruck as if they couldn't believe their perfect plan had met with disaster.

Maggie and Holly both ran to the children checking them for damage. Clearly neither of the women had fully comprehended the reality of the situation.

The little monsters hadn't run away at all!

The police had been called. Maggie had been upset in her delicate condition. Holly had been treated to a second dose of terror over her child going missing. He'd sat and worried for hours with a headache to match the size of the beam that had pounded into his skull. And Trent had been scared to death the whole time that he'd lose another person he loved while he worried about Maggie's health.

And these two had been having a pizza picnic somewhere in the house right under their noses, knowing full well the upheaval they'd caused!

"Where were they?" Jim asked through gritted teeth.

"It seems the third floor of our house has a priest hole between the two playrooms. They have a regular little hideout up there."

Maggie and Holly both backed off staring down at

their little angels as if they'd suddenly sprouted horns. Jim thought perhaps they had!

"What did you two think you were doing?" Jim wanted to know.

"Ian was really scared. His mother threatened to take him all the way back to New Zealand. We had to do something," Rachel explained.

"So you frightened your mothers and tortured your fathers, to what? Pay us back for not doing things your way?" he asked.

"Come on, you three. Come in and join the party," Trent growled and stepped aside, motioning the other children into the kitchen. "Mickey, you can explain how you could let them do this and keep silent. And Daniel can tell me what's wrong with encouraging his little sister to lie for these two. Gracie, you can tell me why you didn't let us know where they were when you saw how afraid Mommy was that they were missing."

Grace's bottom lip quivered. "'Cause if you break a Kids' Club secret, you're in trouble with a cap-it-able *T* and you can't be part of the Kids' Club anymore. I sorry, Daddy." Grace put her pudgy little arms up to Trent, and Jim saw his friend's anger at the littlest Osborne melt into nothingness.

Trent picked her up and hugged her while shooting daggers at his other three over her shoulder. There was clearly still enough fury in his gentle friend to go around.

Daniel looked at Mickey, then away. "Yeah. It's like Grace says. You're dead meat. I didn't want to be dead *or* meat, even though they sounded like the same thing to me.''

Jim thought Trent's head was going to explode the way his eyes widened. He put Grace down next to Daniel. ''You two go up to your rooms and get ready for bed. We'll talk about punishments later.''

''It's hardly even dark yet,'' Daniel was foolish enough to protest.

''Uh, Daniel, I wouldn't push my luck,'' Maggie advised. ''I really think you'd better go on upstairs to your room.''

The two were about three steps from the bottom when Trent whirled toward his two oldest. ''Dead meat?'' he asked.

Jim cleared his throat. ''Might I suggest that we phone the police and call off the dogs as it were. Then I think Holly and I should take little Ian *Dillon*ger over to the apartment and address our grievances with him while you two have a chat with young Bonnie and Clyde here.''

''Sounds like a good idea,'' Maggie agreed, her usually soft brown eyes sharp with anger.

''You two, in the family room. Now,'' Trent told his two. Mickey and Rachel slunk away like condemned prisoners.

Holly remained as silent as she'd been since realizing that Ian had spent the afternoon and evening torturing her while getting regular reports on his success. The anguish in her eyes, however, spoke volumes and turned up Jim's own ire. Ian was in a boatload of trouble.

Jim called the police, who were thrilled that the children had been found. Sergeant Mosby asked to come by to have a chat with the children the next day. Jim, remembering the sergeant he'd met earlier, readily agreed that the big man might just scare the major perpetrators of that day's misdeeds back onto the straight and narrow.

"I'll walk you over to the carriage house," Trent said when Jim got off the phone.

Holly nodded and gestured Ian to the door. "Thanks for all your help, you two. I'll see you tomorrow. Jim, will you be along soon?"

Jim nodded and turned to Trent after Holly left. "I'm a lot steadier on my feet. You stay here and take care of your family. Me and mine have disrupted your lives enough for one day."

Trent and Maggie shared a glance that was packed full of meaning. "You could get disoriented in the dark," Trent said and stepped out on the porch.

Jim followed. The dizziness had passed and his headache had lessened. "This really isn't necessary. I'm fine."

"Physically you seem better, but not emotionally. A couple of years ago you gave me some advice about forgiveness. I wasted a lot of time resisting it. You teach on it all the time. Maybe it's time to listen to your own wisdom."

Jim leaned against the post at the top to the steps. "You seemed pretty angry with Holly yourself."

"She hurt my friend and quite frankly she could have endangered your life by leaving you alone that way. But what she did is understandable in a way. You once left her alone with an infant who couldn't breathe and he almost died. Holly has had reason to doubt you in the past. She was also the kid whose mother fell off the wagon after eight years, so her history with recovered alcoholics is a lot to overcome."

Jim knew he had to forgive Holly. He'd known it all along. That was why he'd had so much trouble trying to pray. Because he'd known what the Lord wanted him to do and he'd been resisting—holding on to his anger. Jim also knew that he'd begged to have Holly in his life and he'd been granted his wish. Now it was up to him to follow God's rules and forgive seventy times seven or he'd never be truly happy.

Chapter Eighteen

Jim stopped at the bottom of the steps to the carriage house. Now that he'd made the decision to forgive Holly, the Lord had shown him that not only had he been unforgiving but he also hadn't been entirely blameless.

He'd been so intent on seeing the day play out the way he'd scripted it that he'd been foolish and stubborn. He'd promised again and again to let God work on Holly's heart, but he'd kept trying to help things along. And he'd been so intent on doing the work of the Lord that he'd nearly undone it. If he'd stayed at the hospital, Holly would have arrived full of concern and love and none of that day's disasters would have happened. And, of course, if he hadn't been wandering around the job site with his head in the clouds, he would have heard the temporary supports crack and gotten out of the way of the falling beam in the first place.

He looked up at the sky. *Please, Lord. I know You have to be getting sick of me forgetting to trust You to handle this but give me one more chance? I promise not to blow it. Please give me the words to say to her.*

Jim moved up a few steps and stopped. Gazing upward again, he muttered aloud, "And the right words to say to Ian would be a big help, too. He was way out of line with this running away nonsense. Political asylum?"

It was a warm night but Holly had the windows open and the air-conditioner off. When he stepped up to the door, he heard Holly say, "Here's your father now."

"Now why does that sound like the follow-up to wait till your father gets home?" he asked as he opened the door.

"Because it is. He wanted to apologize. I made him wait. I'm not the only one he upset with this stunt. Political asylum!"

Jim coughed to cover what had nearly been a snicker. Now that it was all over, he could see the comical elements in the day's drama, but then he remembered Holly wringing her hands and pacing Maggie's kitchen. All levity fled.

"Actually I don't want your apology, Ian. I want an explanation of why you broke a promise to me. You promised me you'd never leave your mother a note and disappear on her the way you did when you came to hear me speak in New York. Do you have any idea how upset your mother and Mrs. Osborne were today, picturing their children walking along narrow country roads then even more dangerous city streets?''

"And did Mickey tell you that your father should have been in hospital all day being watched for complications?'' Holly added. "Do you know the state police were so worried about him that they sent the paramedics to check on him? Do you think the worry did his headache any good?''

Ian had been staring down at the floor, but when he looked up, rather than penitent, he looked happy. "You care about each other again!"

"How your mother and I feel about each other has nothing to do with this!" Jim snapped. "I asked you a question. Why did you break your promise?''

Tears flooded Ian's eyes, but he bit his lip and blinked. "I'm sorry you were both upset, but I had to do something! You were wrecking all our hard work!''

Jim gritted his teeth. "I imagine that is a reference to Operation Wedding Ring. Tell us, what hard work were we wrecking by having a *personal* disagreement."

Ian seemed to know he'd made a grievous misstep. "It—it doesn't matter. Really."

"Oh, it matters plenty," Holly snapped. "Exactly what have you five been up to?''

"Six actually," Ian said then his eyes widened—another misstep.

"I count five," Jim said. "Who was magic number six?''

"Mswhi," Ian mumbled.

"What? I couldn't hear you," Jim demanded, feeling suddenly like a drill instructor.

"Mrs. White," Ian enunciated more carefully.

"The rush vacation?" Jim guessed.

"She thought that perhaps Mum would step into the breach if she left you shorthanded."

"And the accounting? She messed up the books on purpose?" Holly asked, incredulous. Looking at Jim, she added, "She seems like such a sweet innocent lady."

"Oh, Daniel and I did that," Ian assured them. "Daniel's quite a whiz at the computer, as well."

"Why involve Mrs. White?" Jim wanted to know. "I assume she was recruited and didn't volunteer out of the blue."

"You guys weren't ever together. How were you supposed to fall in love and get married again if you never saw each other?"

"I see your point," Jim conceded. *It looks as if You've had more than Your share of help, Lord.* The days at the church working together had brought them closer. Speaking of closer— "What was the point of locking us in that closet?"

"Rachel said it would be romantic and that you'd get to be a hero when you saved Mum."

"Well, it wasn't romantic. It frightened your mother. And speaking of frightening your mother, I think we've gotten off the subject. How could you pull a stunt like you did today after seeing how upset she was when you did it the last time?"

"I was quite desperate," Ian said as if that explained anything.

"And you're going to be quite desperate again. Do you like your room?" Jim asked.

Ian nodded, looking worried. "Yes, sir."

"Oh, that's good because you and your room are going to become really familiar with each other for the next week."

Ian swallowed. "We are?"

"Oh, yeah, because you're going to spend every waking moment in there for the next week. And if for some reason your mother needs to go out, she can drop you at the church and you can have time contemplating the supply closet. And I'll even cut you a break and leave the door open."

"I'm sorry," Ian said again. "Should I go there now?"

Holly looked at Jim, then said. "Oh, I think that would be a terribly smart idea. Now come give us a hug and a kiss. We forgive you, but you mustn't ever do anything like this again. We both love you whether we live together as a family or not."

Ian ran to Holly and hugged her, but when he turned to Jim he approached slowly, clearly not sure of his welcome. Jim dropped to one knee and held out his arms. Ian ran to him then and hugged him fiercely. "Dad," he whispered in Jim's ear. "Was it worth it?"

Jim pulled back and grinned; the kid might be sorry but he clearly thought any success the scheme achieved just might be worth the grounding. Unable to dash the hope he saw in his son's eyes, he leaned forward and put his lips close to Ian's ear. "The ring's in my pocket. I'll let you know."

Ian's arms nearly strangled him before he let go and ran to his room.

"He still looks entirely too pleased with himself," Holly grumbled. She looked at him. "Political asylum?"

Jim snickered. "Where does he get this stuff?"

Holly shook her head. "There are some things under heaven and earth better left unexplored. Listen, I have some cola I could unfizz for you if your stomach is still upset."

"No, thanks. I've had enough caffeine and sugar to keep me going all night."

"Speaking of all night, are you staying at the Osbornes' house? I heard the paramedic tell you not to be alone."

"Yeah," Jim replied, searching for something to say. How could talking to the woman you love suddenly become impossible?

"Is it time for aspirin again?" Holly asked.

Jim sighed. "Holly, let's sit down. We need to talk."

Holly nodded and sat carefully on the edge of the settee. "I don't know how to make you see how sorry I am for misjudging you the way I did. I already apologized to Ian for threatening to take him back to New Zealand."

Jim sat down next to her and leaned back, resting

his head on the back cushion. "Come here," he urged and held out his arms.

As Holly went gratefully into Jim's gentle embrace, she fought tears that burned the back of her throat and her eyes.

"You've already shown me that, sweetheart," he said. "I was wrong not to forgive you right away. Who am I to withhold my forgiveness from you when Christ forgave me for all my sins just for the asking? I've hurt you a lot worse in the past than your misunderstanding my behavior hurt me this afternoon."

"I should have known."

"How? You didn't know I'd been hurt. I realized that I must have looked and sounded drunk."

"Ian knew you were sick."

"And when was the last time Ian was subjected to living with a drunk? You couldn't have known and you had reason to doubt me. Your mother disappointed you after eight years. That must have felt like a lifetime to you back then. And I'm pretty ashamed that Trent had to point it out to me. I'm sorry I wasn't any support for you while we thought the kids were gone."

"I felt so responsible. It was all my fault."

"I blamed you, too. But I was wrong. Ian is responsible for his own actions. Just as you are and as I am."

Holly felt doubly guilty. He shouldn't be accepting responsibility for any wrongdoing. She sat up and twisted to face him. "No. You did nothing to cause that mess. You told me you hadn't been drinking. Why didn't I listen?''

"You answered that already. You were afraid. But, Holly, no one twisted my arm into leaving the hospital. I was determined to convince you to marry me tonight and nothing was going to stop me. Not even getting beamed with a beam.''

Holly's chuckle was a little watery. "I was going to make you dinner and then tell you I'd decided already. You know I'm almost as cross with you for taking such chances with your health as I am with Ian. Honestly, you need a keeper!''

Jim's eyes met hers. "Are you applying for the job?''

Holly froze. He still wanted her. She'd hoped he wasn't just being kind when he'd hugged her, but she'd been afraid to hope.

"That job sounds rather temporary. I'd thought to apply for one with better career opportunities, some fringe benefits and a bit more longevity. You know, something along the lines of wife and mother, a little house in the country and till death do us part.''

Jim pulled her onto his lap and kissed her long and hard. "You're hired.''

Epilogue

Ian watched as his mother and father posed for a picture. Then his mother turned her back to the group of women gathered at the bottom of the steps. His parents were so happy now. It was worth that week during the summer that he'd spent in his room, he mused, just to see them standing there together. A real bride and groom just like on the top of their cake.

"Oh, my goodness!" Mrs. White yelped when the bouquet landed right in her lap, having sailed way past all the ladies who'd really wanted it. His grandfather kissed her hand and she blushed just like his mom always did. His dad had explained the silly superstition about catching the bouquet. He guessed that was why the Mays sisters had been right up there in front.

But Mrs. White caught the bouquet. Did people as old as Grandfather and Mrs. White get married?

"Well, that's the end of Operation Wedding

Ring,'' Mickey said next to him. "We did good, people. Really good."

Ian eyed his mates. "My granddad likes Mrs. White," he said pointedly. If Mickey and Rachel didn't get the idea, he'd drop the whole crazy thing.

But Mickey's eyes narrowed the way they always did when he was thinking—or plotting. "Grandpa George is a lot of fun. If he married Mrs. White, he could stay here. I heard your mom say it was easier for her to stay in the United States because she was getting married."

"And your granddad's going to be at the church taking your dad's place while your parents have their honeymoon and visit Pastor and Mrs. Daniels and baby David," Rachel noted thoughtfully.

"With both Mrs. White and Granddad working at the church every day it should be easy," Ian agreed. "And your mom and dad are so busy with baby Leah that they won't even notice we're up to anything."

"Your granddad'll only be here another month," Mickey reminded him.

"And it took us longer than a month last time," Daniel pointed out.

Rachel smiled. "But they're older and let's face it, they have to make up their minds faster. Hey! I just thought of something! Mrs. White helped your parents fall in love by going away on vacation and now your parents are doing the same thing. Oh, this is so romantic."

"Well, that does it," Daniel groused. "We're in big trouble already."

* * * * *

Dear Reader,

I hope you've enjoyed Jim and Holly's story and the updates on Angel and Greg, Maggie and Trent, and Cassie and Joshua. Jim has intrigued me since the Osborne children ran to greet him in *A Family for Christmas* (12/99). Who was this dynamic young pastor who was as handy with a hammer as he was with a Bible verse? And what was his story? I learned a little more about him while writing *Small-Town Dreams* (5/00), and I couldn't leave him alone and full of regrets. Then I heard about Web pages like the one where Ian found his father, and the solution to Jim's problem seemed obvious.

But he still had things to learn, as did his Holly. As Jim said, letting God work in our lives can be the hardest lesson a Christian must learn. And it should be so easy. Why is it we can trust Him with our salvation, but we can't seem to trust Him to solve our problems? Both Jim and Holly had a hard time with this in different ways. Holly couldn't give up the control over her life that she'd finally achieved and Jim kept trying to help the Maker of the Universe.

I encourage you to give your problems to Him and stop taking them back as Jim did. Believe me, He's a whole lot better a problem solver than you or I will ever be and He truly has our best interests at heart. He is our Savior and His Spirit is our guiding light. We can trust our happiness to Him.

I love hearing from my readers and can be reached at c/o VFRW, P.O. Box 350, Wayne, PA 19087-0350.

Sincerely,

Kate Welsh